I'LL NEVER LEAVE YOU

Also by H. E. Francis

THE INVISIBLE COUNTRY

GOYA, ARE YOU WITH ME NOW?

THE SUDDEN TREES

A DISTURBANCE OF GULLS

HAD

THE HISTORY OF A MAN IN DESPAIR

THE ITINERARY OF BEGGARS

NAMING THINGS

CINCO MILLAS HASTA DICIEMBRE, Y COMO LOS PECES, COMO LOS PAJAROS, COMO LA HIERBA

TODA LA GIENTE QUE NUNCA TUVE

I'LL NEVER LEAVE YOU

STORIES

H. E. FRANCIS

Winner of the
G. S. Sharat Chandra Prize for Short Fiction
Selected by Diane Glancy

BkMk Press
University of Missouri-Kansas City

BkMk Press
University of Missouri-Kansas City
5101 Rockhill Road
Kansas City, Missouri 64110
(816) 235-2558 (voice)
(816) 235-2611 (fax)
www.umkc.edu/bkmk
bkmk@umkc.edu

Cover design: Nicole Bentley
Author photo: N. L. Romero
Managing Editor: Ben Furnish
Assistant Managing Editor: Susan L. Schurman

BkMk Press wishes to thank the following individuals for editorial and production assistance: Bill Beeson, Dennis Conrow, Linda Rodriguez, Tom Russell, Elizabeth Smith.

The G. S. Sharat Chandra Prize for Short Fiction is given in memory of Chandra, who was a professor of English at the University of Missouri-Kansas City until his death in 2000. The prize was previously awarded to Ron Tanner for his book *A Bed of Nails*, selected by Janet Burroway.

Printing by Technical Communications Services, North Kansas City, Mo.

Library of Congress Cataloging-in-Publication Data

Francis, H. E. (Herbert Edward).
I'll never leave you : stories / H. E. Francis.
v. cm.
Contents: The playground – Boulders – The winter guest – The private lives of children – I'll never leave you – Watching Marie – Battered shore – Lib – Minor matters.
ISBN 1886157472
1. Psychological fiction, American.
2. Loss (Psychology)—Fiction.
3. Atlantic Coast (U. S.)—Fiction.
PS3556.R328 I15 2004
813/.54 22 2004015356
CIP

To

NORBERTO LUIS ROMERO

to

RAMIRO FERNANDEZ FERNANDEZ

and to

CARLOS AND MARTA DE LA ROSA

Acknowledgments

"The Playground" was published in *Shenandoah*, "The Boulders" in *Five Fingers Review*, "The Winter Guest" in *Alaska Quarterly Review*, "The Private Lives of Children" in *Ontario Review*, "Watching Marie" in *The Bridge*, "The Battered Shore" in *Southwest Review*, "Lib" in *Mānoa*, and "Minor Matters" in *Cimarron Review*.

I like the solid stories of H. E. Francis and the more experimental, "turned loose" writing that marbles the collection. There are haunting characters caught in the web of tight prose. There is a frequency of memorable lines: "Dark had absorbed the woods and they could see only themselves in the panes" and "Words are the last stand against oblivion." It's the relationship of characters, the fluid imagery, the lyric quality that holds the reader. The dog, Edge, in "I'll Never Leave You," the family dynamics in "The Battered Shore," the stream of consciousness in "The Private Lives of Children," the impact of "Watching Marie." Yes, these are stories that don't leave.

—Diane Glancy
Judge, G. S. Sharat Chandra Prize for Short Fiction

Contents

THE PLAYGROUND

For Manuel Rivas

From the window Rolfe said, There she is.

They had grown accustomed.

The woman came along the beach to the playground. When they saw her, all the children shouted, ran, and gathered about her like chicks. You could see her head thrown back in laughter. The children, Julia's—Ben and Raula—said she didn't have to say a word. Her hands told all they needed to know.

From the house, which faced the playground on the sand, Julia and Rolfe and Evan could keep an eye on the children. Things happened on the water. After Labor Day, the beach was abandoned. Only wind stirred the swings. But, since the woman, they no longer worried about the children.

They watched—Evan from his study upstairs, Julia from the front room, Rolfe form the bedroom el. So little happened here, but she happened.

Weekdays, as if prearranged now, she appeared after school hours; and, as if she were one, in an instant she was moving with the children.

What's she doing now?

They're all doing it, Julia said. Because all were moving in a circle about her, one child rising as the woman's left arm rose slowly, one sinking as her right sank, each alternately rising and falling as a fluttering live corolla, a sea anemone breathing on the show.

Beautiful! Evan said.

Magic, Julia murmured. It made her touch Rolfe. He stared, surprised, at her hand.

She comes to town and in no time they're eating out of her hand.

The woman had come for the winter. She had come for sea, and cold, and snow. Through Bick's agency, she or someone for her had taken the Tabor house, built by the painter, dead three years now, the house usually rented summer but winter abandoned. Since little happened here, the woman was an instant curiosity, sudden in the village: not young but far from old, with fast legs, a real walker, and what Julia called a chiseled face, firm and squarish with a sort of Slavic austerity, the eyes with a glitter of dark fire filling her placid face with sudden life. She wore what looked like heavy homemade turtlenecks under a navy wool mackinaw, and a navy knitted hat.

Bick must have arranged the rental long distance, Rolfe said. She came with almost noting, accompanied by a man who settled her in, stayed the weekend, and left. Must do everything herself. Nobody else is there. Nobody goes.

Of course, Julia and Rolfe and Evan argued. Always, Evan said, we're at each other's throat, he the least discursive if not always the least antagonistic, mostly about work, because on Julia depended the upkeep of the house, with no man now, her good-for-nothing husband gone and meanly avoiding *decent* work to avoid child support, stubborn because he wanted Julia back, but her answer: Never in this world. Rolfe said, You were better off when he *was* here. How would *you* know when a woman's better off?" Julia said. Tell me. Rolfe said, Oh, I *could* tell you. Tell me, then—go ahead, tell me. But Rolfe was silent and truned to Evan for support, if he'd give it, *not* very frequently; but Julia said, If you knew anything about women, you wouldn't be here, would he, Evan? As Evan kept silent—unusual for him—she said, You're two of a kind. Now, Evan said, you're going too far. Well, *you* could get work too, Julia said. Work! You don't call writing a book work? You've *been* writing that book since—Genesis! You'd think, Julia, *I* didn't have any more right in this house than you and Rolfe. Remember, this place belongs to all of us, or why'd *you* move back in after the *disaster* with *him*! Julia bit. It always came down to that, the house, this house, the inheritance the three would never agree on splitting by selling it. And why wouldn't Julia move in? Where else could she go with two children? How many men would take a woman with somebody else's children? And Ben and Raula were such fine children. They were their bond—at least she and her brothers agreed on that.

But, though they did disagree, when they first saw the strange woman, their attentions focused on her. That first afternoon they thought her clothes strange: a shawl of some kind with a bulky knot over her mackinaw and her head done up in a kind of bandana, since replaced but the knitted hat; so they could actually see no hair but quite clearly see that—Julia called it—sculptured face. Yes, they had agreed, curiosity quite aroused, forgetting how they might be so obviously perceived standing together now, faces as if fused in the window, baldly gawking. That lady halted on the playground, faced the sea long, strangely still, and then turned, sat on a swing, and eased back and forth for the longest time as the three speculated: She's foreign, no doubt about that, Evan said. Why foreign? I mean her faced could be any Polack's in town. We've plenty of them here. But her clothes, Evan said. Made in America, Rolfe went ironic. O-kay! Evan said, so who can tell these days? *I* can, Julia said. It's her way of walking, her poise, her reactions—they all say *Not from here*. Now you're being intuitive, Rolfe said. Why not? I'm a woman. Besides, intuition works, doesn't it? Rolfe said, You *say*. But they went on: A recluse. A divorcée. An artist. A political escapee. An exile. Maybe just a loner—some people are. Or recuperating from a serious illness. Julia broke their meanderings: Or a writer—with a job. You *would*, Evan said, but actually laughing at her inference as they went on watching.

Almost at once, the stranger had discovered the children, Ben and Raula and their usual playmates from school, Les and Bella, their nearest neighbors here at the edge of the village. And, if at first their parents' curiosity was piqued by her presence in town, the children goaded it further: Theirs was "the day of the lady," eyes brilliant with anticipation, mouths going incessantly. She's magic, Raula cried. The woman's hands made creatures, made birds, made shadows fly over the sand as the children made bird language. And Ben: Her hands tell things. And Raula: She makes you *know* what to do. And what does she say? Say? Oh, talk would spoil it; she makes sounds we understand.

Foreign, then.

Oh, in now time every day after school they stopped hardly long enough to drop off their packs and shot across to the playground, almost desperate she might not appear. But appear she did, exactly at 3:30, they soon learned, striding along the sand from the Tabor house on the promontory, her daily exercise no doubt, capped by a good strenuous hour before supper and her striding off, vital, gradually shrinking, made even smaller as she approached the monolithic boulders at the point.

Soon the three—Evan and Rolfe and Julia if she came home early from work at the real estate office—veered toward the front windows with increasing frequency.

They were startled when Raula said, She tells us what to do.

Tells, Julia said. How? Julia said.

With *words*, Ma

But you said she didn't speak English.

She doesn't.

Then you understand?

Of course!

Not words, Raula! *Sounds*, Ben said.

But they're *her* words, Ben.

Yes.

Hers? Julia said.

Because sometimes she makes them to the water or a cloud or the sand, Ben said.

Raula said, Like she forgot the game—and then remembers us. And laughs. It makes us all laugh.

That's just part of the *game*, Raula! Ben said.

But Julia knew the children had that aptitude for instinctive understanding, dead in the three, in most adults.

Evan said, She shops at the IGA. I ran into her. Actually, I sort of followed her around. Vegetables. Lots of them. After, she crossed to the docks and stood by a piling and looked a long time at the boats and the water. Then—imagine!—she walked with her groceries all the way from downtown—from the harbor, up Main to the back road and through the woods to the promontory—and in this cold. She's certainly robust.

Don't tell me you didn't—

As a matter of fact, I did offer a ride. But she waved her arm No, but with a grateful smile, beautiful. She has a really impressive face, strong.

Well, she's certainly given *you* an interest.

And not you?

Well, not the same kind. Julia smiled. What you need.

Now, now. We won't start again, will we?

But Evan, to make himself a familiar sight, sometimes stood outside the house to watch them at play. At times Rolfe too went out and walked the beach, keeping distance. Above all, Julia said, we mustn't upset her. It would be a crime to spoil the children's expectations.

Children's because now, most of the time, the woman had eight usuals and one or two occasionals.

She is magic.

Because the woman made the children fluid, blended them, but gave each his own life. Julia was startled at how many selves they seemed to bring home.

Look, Evan—they must be playing something like statues. But then the woman's arms directed motion and they were playing out a scene. Sometimes they would stand in a close circle back to back, a stem with eight faces, then run a certain number of steps, halt, kneel, throw their heads back and sway in unison, a single great living creature. And sometimes dance, each making little twirls and then moving slowly toward one another and then away, like long, slow breaths.

At 4:30 precisely, with dark coming on, she would retreat, wave herself off. They would cry Bye after her and stand an instant watching—almost a silent lament—before turning to the house, suddenly laughing and shouting, Tomorrow. See you at school.

Of course they—town, in fact—were curious. Who was she? What? After the first two weeks, on a Friday a van drove up. Whoever, the man left on Sunday—and returned every second Friday.

Because of its location on a promontory, with a long dirt driveway through a wood, the house was not visible from the road—from the beach, yes—and because it was winter few roamed the beach or rowed or set out lobster pots, so it was some time before anyone knew that the woman had actually come to paint until a water heater went bad and she walked to town to Bick's with whom the owners of the Tabor house had a contract. So it was Larry Brooks who, in a passing glimpse of the studio, first reported easels and canvases.

The local gallery in the old antique stores remodeled to attract tourists was animated by the idea of someone perhaps exceptional, even known, who might exhibit, with some extensive publicity, and enliven the winter; and she *had* passed and halted to view island landscapes in the showcase windows, but did not enter—and, on inquiry, the gallery learned of her language problem, insisting, however, that art spoke beyond language. But before anyone approached her, the gallery learned that the van of whoever it was who came every two weeks was seen parked briefly on Front Street in the village—there were paintings in it.

It was Evan, as a writer more than curious, who kept notes on the woman to preserve perhaps for a character profile, or something like that, he said, though at first Rolfe thought him presumptuous, a busybody, worse than an old woman; but, instead of arguing as always, Evan merely said, Well, there's a little of the woman in every man and more in most writers. I'll buy that, Rolfe said without the usual irony.

So when the kids talked, Evan—they all—"collected" tidbits.

Raula said, She sees things in the clouds.

What things?

Things!

How do you know?

Because her face.

What about her face?

It hurts.

Hurts?

Yes.

That's part of the *game*, Raula! Ben said.

So Evan spent more time watching: how the woman turned child—he could believe she *was* one—from her motions, expressions, her face a momentary innocence which with an abrupt tilt of her head turned stone, as if shaped by centuries of wind.

And once, after the children had come in because of heavy snow and the woman halted, Julia, opening the window a bit, heard sounds that might have come from her own throat, taut sounds, agony, not sounds she had experienced but *knew*. Not part of the game. The heavy snow coming down made the woman spectral and only the voice was alive.

But Julia—the three were sitting around the kitchen table—said, I think she *needs* the children.

Needs?

Because she's so regular and she so obviously puts such love into the games.

She understands them, Evan said. I mean—you've seen it, you've *said* it enough—with them she turns into a child.

But then—suddenly—she's *not*. You've seen that.

It was Rolfe who said, Something breaks in and hurts her. I can identify with that. So can you two. We've had . . . well, enough of that.

But have you *heard* her? Evan said.

You too? Julia said.

When she's alone sometimes—oh, not long, but just before the children come, sometimes after if they hurry off first. I've been outside—it hurts me to hear her; but she, really, flees from any approach. She's hard to figure.

Wait, Rolfe said. Let her be. If she needs, or wants, anyone, she'll let somebody know. We could all do that, couldn't we?

Well, if we don't *start*! At least *you* haven't lately. Meaning: answering complaints about his not working with—Well, you're living in my—part of my—house too. Doesn't that count for money?

Okay, but let's *don't*, Evan said, sensitive about his, at this point anyway, non-paying piled-up pages.

Weekends, regularly, the woman did not come. Julia understood from others that she walked in the other direction. Because there's no school, Julia said. She knows weekends are for family. She must be lonely. After all, she doesn't know anyone.

Well, somebody, Rolfe said. That man in the van.

But family or no, Ben and Raula fretted. They crossed to the playground, hung by the swings. Sulked. Bickered. Pestered. Let's do a snowman, Rolfe said, but they had no enthusiasm. The matinee? Evan offered. Or walk into town? They too, the three, looked out at the white landscape, bleak, feeling its emptiness.

Weeks went that way. Only Sunday nights the brightness came back into the children: Monday tomorrow, Raula cried, Monday, Ben, Monday! They were two pigeons cooing.

And as faithful as Monday, she was there, and Mondays slipped into months till in late March, unexpected, all heaven seemed to fall—white, white, deep and still. The woman did not come. And they would not let the children out for a long time.

But what of *her*? Julia said.

Her, Evan echoed.

Yes, Rolfe said. For the bare unblemished show, deep, caused all three to miss the regularity, as if, afternoons, their bodies were drawn instinctively toward the light and sand and sea, expectant.

She— Miss...

Her name's Lady, Ben said.

Lady! That can't be her name.

We call her that, Raula said, and she likes it, so that's her name. She smiles when we say it. *So there.*

Now, now, don't get smart.

On weekends Raula and Ben, their routine broken, were hard to tame.

The woman can't get out in this, Evan said. Anything could happen. Somebody's got to—I will—drive out to the Tabor Place.

No, Julia said, let me.

We'll both go—or all three?

I don't think that's wise, Evan.

It's safer with three than one.

No, it's not that—it's the children. She's a woman—I mean, I think she'll feel more comfortable, from the way she is with them, with a woman.

Julia's right. Rolfe's tone was nonetheless dubious.

If I could take the children....

You can't. She's painting, Raula said.

However do you know that?

We were there.

Were there! When?

Before the snow.

Raula! Ben! You never *told* us.

She took you to the Tabor house? Evan said.

She *didn't* take us.

You mean you followed her?

W e just went. Saturday. We sat outside and waited.

What for?

For her to see us.

Why, Ben! Raula! You know you're never supposed to wander off, or follow anybody, *ever.*

And did you go in? Evan said.

Sure, Ben said.

Then what?

She gave us milk and let us watch her paint.

What? Evan said, meaning what she painted.

Just faces, Ben said.

Lots, Raula said.

What kind of faces?

Like ours. Kids' I mean.

No, Ben, they're older.

Kids'! Ben said.

That does it. Julia rose. I'm going alone. She'll be more comfortable with me, surely. I'll take the station wagon.

You're sure? Rolfe said. I could drive—and wait outside.

I won't be long. If I'm not back in an hour, come with the Chevy.

On the road the snow was deep, but still fluffy, slippery, not damp hard and glazed over yet, and as she had only to stay on Main and turn at the North Road, not far from the Tabor entrance, and drive though the woods to the house. . . . She was relieved at the dirt road under thick trees, virtually a tunnel to the house in the green seasons, somewhat cut off the heavy fall of snow. She came out behind the kitchen. Since the front, high on the bluff, gave onto the ocean, fearing the woman might not hear or see the van, she pressed the horn several times and waited with the motor running.

The back door was abruptly opened and the woman stood nonplussed a moment, but then—surely recognizing her as Ben and Raula's mother—gave a broad smile and flagged her in. Once she approached the door, the woman silently gestured *Come.*

And at her silence instantly it struck Julia clearly—she can't talk!—why the children never once had come home and said, The lady *said.*

The woman gestured *Sit?* Julia nodded and sat; and the woman indicated, imitating sipping and the kettle, perhaps tea or coffee; and Julia said, Yes, but touched her watch and said, I have to keep an eye on the time, my brothers will be worried, and added, Because of the snow, her hand scooping unconsciously toward the snow. The woman seemed to understand and put on a bit of water, and as they waited for the kettle to whistle, the woman's fingers went to her open mouth as if to extract her tongue, her voice, and throw it off. . . . Gone? Lost? *Yes.*

The kitchen was nearly bare. Julia could hardly conceal her startle at the emptiness; no curtains, not even a shade, nothing but a few dishes in a bare cupboard, the snow pouring light in, making everything white, bright, too white. But the woman, surely seeing her consternation, set down her tea (were there only two cups? One for that visitor?) and beckoned her farther in—through a central passageway past open doors, two empty rooms, then another pair of empty rooms; and suddenly she was standing high in all light, space you might fall into, the sweep of sea, she might have been *on* the sea; but the room itself was a sudden chaos—low tables, small pots, cans, oils, tubes, canvases, two easels, a table laden with brushes and instruments, a chaos suggesting a frenzy of work; and paintings tilted lined the walls, and no furniture but a daybed. At sight of the canvasses, *Ohhhh!* Julia uttered, too startled to know whether joy? pain? and glanced at the woman, who smiled and nodded, who must have understood her emotion because *children, children.* The woman spread her arms, *Look*, showing her, her eyes filled, but smiling; and Julia's own filled and she reached for the woman's hand and felt the woman's clutch hers, so warm, and for the briefest instant they stood together, staring into each other, as if what was in the paintings Julia was seeing reflected in the woman, those children's faces spilling from her eyes.

Julia cold hardly contain the vision:

Faces. Children's. Faces of children growing like blossoms out of scattered arms, legs, breasts, skulls; out of hands; out of guns; out of bones; faces floating in red puddles, growing from red pools; faces in lilies and roses and chrysanthemums with fine vines red as blood winding up into them.

Under were bones, under were bodies rotting to bone, cadavers, skeletons. Some were mounds of bones, some piles of tiny bones, canvases of bones, and out of bones grew stems and garlands of children's faces green yellow violet orange blue pink; and red rain falling, and horrific, crawling creatures with human faces gnawing at the stems or with infinite tiny red tongues extended for the falling red rain.

And in some of the faces, Julia saw reflections of Ben and Raula and Suzie, Manny, Bella, Les; and when she turned her inquiring gaze to the woman, her hand went to her breast and she said, *Mine?* The woman nodded. And Julia said, *Yours?* And the woman touched her own breast. *Yes*. Then the woman spread her arms, swept them out—out there, over water, out, out. And if for an instant confused, Julia realized: Everybody's? *Yes.* She nodded vigorously.

Finally Julia said, I'm Julia. *Jul*-ia. And you're—she smiled complicitously—*La*-dy.

At the familiar sound of the children's name for her, she smiled, opened her mouth and made sounds in response, but nothing, no words, then raised her hand—Wait—and in an instant, on heavy drawing paper, with a fine brush, in sky blue she wrote *Nadya Bogdanavich.*

Julia pronounced it, and as if moved, grateful for just the sound of her own name, her language, her throat made a kind of laughter, she clutched Julia's arm and nodded like Pronounced perfect.

But they had not touched the tea, and they sat and Julia took a few sips and they sat in silence awhile and then Julia showed her watch and swept her arm at the snow and indicated Back, my brothers, the children. The woman nodded, knew.

At the car, Julia waved.

Driving down the dirt road, she saw the woman stand long in the doorway with her arm still raised.

At the house Evan said, Tell us, and Ben and Raula plagued to know would Lady come.

But she did not come, and after the long cold spell, with the snow turned slush and then melted, they learned from Bick's that the woman had left, though he did not know where, as the man had left no forwarding address.

The mystery held them. The three, evenings, liked to speculate. They turned curious about *out there.* Feeling for Ben and Raula, in spare time Evan crossed to the playground; and Rolfe, having gotten on at the lumber company part-time, invented games with them.

And bit by bit, at leisure, Julia repeatedly laid out her visit, in detail, for Evan and Rolfe—recalling what she had seen that she had since dwelled painfully on: That woman's isolation was too much, surely not chosen but necessary, the isolation in that house, in that language, in this language.

They speculated, then, the three. Whatever had happened to her, something had taken her speech! What she must have experienced! Who can imagine?

And what lost, Julia said, and won't let die.

She could see now—out there, in the sky—those children's

faces, face after face, frail and still beautiful but with an innocence darkened by sudden maturity.

Those children, she said.

If she could only have told us, Evan said.

Some things are too deep to tell, she said.

Yes, Rolfe said. Anyway, she can't tell us.

But, Julia murmured, she does.

THE BOULDERS

A thousand times she had tried to imagine him her son Ran in that city she didn't know, on that street, in the house she had never seen but knew, oh yes knew, how she knew it! It assaulted her from the TV news and photo after photo in the newspapers. She knew the bed and chair and table, the wall of photos of great men he must have read and admired, even loved, whose words he lived by or distorted and died by. She knew the dead girls' faces, the unearthed remains, the graves, the woods that he must have roamed and known intimately, where he must have followed or lured them, assaulted, raped, slaughtered, buried them. But her imagination halted at the woods' edge. The son she *saw*, the boy she knew who would always in her mind be the boy who had gone years before to that city she had never seen but knew—for her that street, that house, that room would be all that city to her, forever complete in her mind. She who had lived all her life by the sea, who could not exist without the sight of the Sound and sand and white stones and those primordial boulders that stood like a strangely scattered stonehenge on the beach below her house on the sand cliff, who knew Paris and Rome and London and Buenos Aires and Madrid and Berlin and Rio de Janeiro and year after year New York City, knew no city like this one she had never seen. Newspapers and TV had taken her into that city and she could never get out. That city was her son. She was inside her son. She could know no more of him, and she could not batter her way out. She could only imagine what was *inside* him. She could never stop imagining. She could not help it. She had to. She was what he was. She was who he was.

Mine.

Me.

The Rockford Killer.

The mother of the Rockford Killer.

How does it feel to be the mother of a killer?

After the execution and then a long surcease of what had seemed an unending persistence of newsmongers, she thought her own curiosity had gone dead, but this one—young he was—had aroused it. Three days he had appeared on the beach below, too late for swimming and with no rowboat or lobster pots or fishing equipment. Each day he had halted a good distance from the house and stood staring at it for a long while, then left. What lingered was that image of him so small against the boulders beyond. So small. Helpless looking. Ran she thought of. Small too. Helpless. In that cell *where he belonged* till the punishment *which he deserved*. She had come to think in those automatic, made phrases that revealed nothing. Who belonged? And where? What was deserved? Why? How?

The next time she saw the boy she was in town in the IGA. She was sure it was that boy, though at close range he was more man than boy.

Lily Cooper was there. She hadn't exactly ducked into the next aisle but turned her head to the cereals and fingered the boxes. She herself had long since developed the habit of practicing some mercy on people by keeping her eye on her cart or shelves or floor to avoid embarrassing them or to avoid their—she could hear them—*embarrassing poor Minna*. Actually Lily was little different from most of the town. Except for the few they were distant if superficially friendly, evasive but when unavoidably confronted polite, always *socially* sympathetic, and when cornered would talk of course about the economy, local tourism, the weather, her work at the law office. Tom had been absolutely loyal in wanting to keep her on, but—and she *did* pity him with all her heart—for months after Ran's capture newsmongers had invaded and made office life wretched for him—so she finally resigned for Tom and *for his family's sake* despite Tom and Sue's objections. But Tom had not for a minute abandoned her. Sue—or anybody else—might have seen his car at the house, difficult unless they got far enough off the road to see up her long driveway to the Sound cliff.

Tom was a strength. She could talk. She could go fluid with words and he would never cut her off. He was brilliant, analytical, nonjudgmental. He won a high percentage of cases; when he lost, he probed his failure, gained knowledge, nothing was wasted on him. In the early years, if she hadn't married Josh, she'd have yielded to Tom. She had loved *her Jew* till the day he was killed on a business flight to Lisbon. And she loved the sterling Tom. No husband could have been a better friend. He could manage an indifferent air in any kind of confrontation, an ability that discouraged contention. Tom—and her experience in the law office—sustained her; so she could bear the town. The god she thanked was Tom. There were a few others, immensely kind, who would call and visit and without pitying or condescending or patronizing her—not treating her as if nothing had happened, but showing that nothing had made any difference to their relationship. Throughout it all any such thought as *I could have died* had nothing to do with her and all to do with *him, Ran, my son.* Yes, she would have died for him. She had no thought of her own death embarrassment disgrace. All she could think of was his life and death and, more, who he was, what. If she could know.

If I could know.

After seeing him in town, the boy, man, appeared on the beach watching the house again. She began to expect him, watched for him. Invariably he came. *I should be afraid.* She wasn't afraid. The worst had happened. What else could matter? Her life? What *was* her life? or life? If he wanted hers—why would he? anybody?—he was slow about it. He looked as helpless down on the beach as she felt up here at the house. Tom she told about it.

Tom wanted the police to question him. But she had absolutely no evidence he was after her or anything in the house. It *appeared* so. Suspicion is enough for questioning. Wait. She wanted more to go on. I have an intuition, but I don't know what. But Tom, she saw, was worried.

The next morning she watched. When the boy appeared she went down. She walked the beach straight to where he was. She made no bones about it. She said This is what you wanted, isn't it?

He gazed directly, candidly, at her.

You're his mother.

His.

The wind seemed to take her breath.

You're his mother.

She nodded finally.

I'm Minna Shusman.

When he offered nothing, she said, Who are you?

I'm his brother.

His brother? I don't understand.

You don't understand?

Then she did. OhmyGod, *his*. And as quickly as she thought *his*, his murdered brother, she thought *Ran*, she *saw* Ran, her eyes filled, *injection*, her heart seemed to swell and fill her, *lethal*, and she felt what the boy must be feeling for his brother, she closed her eyes just a moment, swaying she felt, but it was deceptive, the wind pressing and pressing.

Mark Ridley is your brother, she said.

My brother, yes. Was.

She couldn't speak.

He was all I had, my brother.

She stared at him.

All I had, she said. She could freeze still, die. He was all I had, she repeated. The words were so quiet, but her blood, something, was crying out with this boy's silent cries. She *must* not. She was trembling.

But—? She did not understand. What do you want—here?

I want him back, he said, my brother.

But—that's impossible.

She thought *I cannot bear more madness, I can't.*

I know that's impossible—do you think I'm a fool?—but I had to see what made the man who took my brother and—

Don't! she thought.

He did not. What he was seeing was too horrible. It would be too horrible for both of them, forever.

You mean me?

I mean you, this place, anybody, anything . . . to help me explain what *he* was and in that way bring my brother back . . . .

He.

Ran, you mean. My son. Randolph Shusman.

Him, yes.

Say it.

Say it?

His name. He had one. He was a person.

How can you—?

A person, she said, staring down his belligerence. He grew pensive. Had she startled him? Did he see *she* was a person too?

Randolph Shusman, he said. Perhaps it was the first time he had ever uttered the name.

What *she* saw was how the impulse to kill reverberated: Had it roused an incipient impulse in him to the point of obsession?

Randolph Shusman, she said. She was shaken. She turned and left him standing on the sand and went back to the house.

He's Mark Ridley's brother, she told Tom.

What's he want?

He's not sure. He has to pursue it, that's obvious.

We can do something to protect you. He may be dangerous.

No, no. I'm sure he's not.

How can you be sure?

Intuition, she said.

Intuition! Minna, listen, anything could happen.

He's not bad, I'm sure of that.

You can't be. If anybody . . . well, you understand what I'm saying.

Of course. Ran. You can never be sure. I was always so sure of Ran.

He was silent.

You understand . . . everything, she said.

Too little, he said. You're sure, then, he's not a menace.

Not sure, no. I don't *feel* he is. But I'll go on that. For all I know he may realize the futility of what he's doing and disappear.

Don't count on it, not if he's come all this way.

What she *had* counted on during the whole of the long nightmare was distance, to protect her from reporters: This town on the tip of the north fork of Long Island was not the easiest place to get to.

But they had come, and now *he* had.

For days after their confrontation on the beach, he did not appear. Was that some kind of strategy? Because whenever she looked down at the beach, his figure stood, unshakeable. It was there, but not. And she waited. She found herself expecting him. That talk had made her mind spill what she had struggled so long to contain, and she had repeats of those nights when numb you see numb those pictures passing over your eyes unceasingly without any comprehension as to why they come and come and come, and then suddenly comes a moment when they pass over your eyes with such intense intimacy my son my son my son that you believe *you* are doing it *you* are assaulting raping killing burying and cannot stop you cannot stop you cannot stop Ran him you.

Then late one afternoon she looked out and the boy was down on the sand. She did not expect him at that hour. *Had* he been there every day at that time? At dark he left.

Did he come back nights?

Was that part of his strategy, to remind you that you're the killer's mother?

What does he want here?

What does he want of me?

Tom said You mean he's staying in town!

She said He's got a job here—with the lumber company. I

met him downtown. He was eating at the Coronet. It was his lunch break. He needs the money, he said, he's broke.

That doesn't say much for him. You want me to talk to Brig about him?

No. The truth is . . . I'm curious. He's done that to me. We don't know a thing about him. Besides, if you think he's trouble, dangerous, getting him fired would certainly set him off.

I think, she said, he wants me to get used to seeing him in town. He makes no effort to see me or to come to the house. Of course he's on the beach always at the same hour.

That's intimidation, Tom said.

But he never comes any closer.

Worse. He may be trying to keep you in a state of anxiety, making you wonder *when* he'll break his pattern.

Then he's failed.

That doesn't mean he doesn't think that way, Tom said.

Or that he does. You always say see both sides—and . . . talking to him—oh, I *know* you can't judge by appearances, voice, but—if he was lonely, confused, even desperate because of his brother—he *wants* his brother, he said, though I'm not sure what he meant by it—still, there was something tender . . . in how he said . . . in his voice, his eyes even . . . .

I can't trust that, Minna.

Because you're a lawyer. I'm just a woman.

She laughed.

Well, that's a good sign at least.

What, that I'm just a woman?

No. You're laughing.

Who was it who said laughter is prayer?

It was windy and cloudy, the kind of late October day she liked to walk the beach, moody. She never tired of the shifting sand, stones, the mesmerizing waves, the relentless suck and heave. When she rounded the point, where the boulders abounded, she saw him sitting hunched on the shore and she halted—he didn't see her—and then went on; but, much later, on the way back he was waiting.

She said It's a quiet town. You don't miss home?

Home?

Isn't Rockford home?

I'm just as at home here.

But you don't know anybody here! Aren't you lonely?

I've been lonely since Mark—I was there because of him. He had scholarships to Chicago, he was a teaching fellow at the university, and though he was older I worked from the beginning to help get him through. He was brilliant, he was worth it, everything, and I wasn't such a hot student. So when he . . . Why would I stay in Rockford? He was gone. I had nothing. What do you do when your purpose is gone? I wanted some connection. It was too hard to do without him. I handed over Mark's work, his papers, to his university advisor, Professor Mann, and left. I headed for the only person still connected to him. You see?

He was staring at her.

No, she said. But she saw.

I came straight to you.

But I never knew your brother!

No, but your son did, and you're still here, and I am. It makes me believe. It gives me something.

Gives you . . .?

Don't ask me. I don't know what. I just know you're connected, it's changed your life forever, you can never get away from my brother because he's tied to your son's life, and yours, for good, and that's enough reason, isn't it? To begin with, I had to be near this town. You.

Me?

I had to start somewhere.

With then . . . the murderer's mother. Is that it?

With this place.

But not me?

No. With you. Whatever's part of the place. And his life.

You want to explain something to yourself? Understand?

And to you too maybe. I'm not sure.

At the boulders Ralph told her: It was a rooming house, except for the basement apartment my brother and I had since he'd started his work on the Ph.D. I worked in the factory shipping department where your son worked—you'll know some of this—though I didn't know him, nobody did. He was a good worker, serious, concentrated—a brain, they used to kid. He could do anything he wanted to, but they didn't know, they had no reason to say so, or maybe because of his name, Jewish, because so many Jews are so smart, but Shusman never said a word, once maybe, the time I'm telling you about, only it never struck me till long after everything was over, the way a few words hit like lightning too late and you slap your leg and say Jesus, that's it! It was impulse one night when Mark stayed over from Chicago and I said Mark I'm in the mood for pizza. I never liked to keep him away from his work too long, but insisted—it was Friday—and insisted he relax *sometime*. He laughed. It was the *sometime* got him. Shusman came in the pizzeria just as we sat down. I—it was my great mistake—introduced my brother. I'm the guilty one. If I hadn't, he'd be here now.

You can't take the blame for that.

But I do. I'm guilty. That's my part in it.

Your part?

Yes. We all have our part. You don't? He's yours, isn't he? Anyway, I said Come on, sit with us or Do you mind if we join you? He just slid over in the booth. We sat opposite him. *Now* it's easy to see he didn't like that—he wasn't unpleasant, cold maybe, when I think back. Of course I'd have had no reason to be thinking any of this at the time, but I've thought of almost nothing else *but*, since. Shusman never did talk much, but my brother's the world's best talker. My brother's very perceptive, was, and saw right into people—he'd have made a great lawyer, but criminology, that's where he was headed: and he had theories, but based on lab work, case studies. He never stopped working. My brother could talk about anything and did, though with his head so full of cases he could go on talking about his work for hours. And Shusman seemed very interested, such a good listener that my brother asked why he'd given up study. It was then he said, *I've got a one-track mind*. But my brother didn't let him off. He laughed. So did Jesus, he said, and so did Judas. That launched Mark into his theories. Shusman was totally involved—my brother's talk gets you like that—though he said almost nothing. He even looked spellbound. Now it's easy to see he had been so spellbound he must already have been planning to kill Mark—he *must* have had to have a strong reason to interrupt the string of girls he'd killed to kill a man and this time not for sex—that was the mystery, nobody could figure it out, and it never occurred to me, *I* never connected that meeting with any reason why he'd murder Mark until I'd gone mad with thought and thought. Like everything else simple, or maybe it wasn't, after so much saturation it hit suddenly. How could Mark know that the man he was talking to had killed six girls? Anyway, for Mark and me it was just another pizza and more talk but as I see it now, for Shusman it must have been terrible, he must have had to work hard not to show an excessive interest or ask questions or reveal a possible paranoia. He knew Mark was staring right at a murderer and maybe even imagined Mark either suspected or knew it. An obsession can govern every minute of your life, Mark said. It's not for nothing that men have set Jesus and Judas face to face—even the names, two Js, the syllables, number of letters seem contrived to stand for something more when you think about the men, what they did, our nature itself, life: one obsessed with an idea he lived for, the kingdom of God is within you, and the other confronting it, two sides of the same core in ourselves pictorialized in those two men, in any two men or in any man when the impulses war with each other. Saints and devils. The saint and devil in each of us, when pushed to the extreme. One arouses the other, a Hitler arouses a Churchill. In each case it takes a madness to rouse and provoke itself to defend itself, save itself, to face its own madness and redirect it. But for some that's impossible. Why? Because not only their irrational impulses are directed undeviatingly toward one end, but even the reason has no other purpose than to guide that irrational impulse to fulfill its purpose. He never thinks of anything else but that impulse. What it means is that that person is simple. Simple? In this sense: that he shuns any complexity because he cannot handle it; he shunts everything into that one impulse which is so dominant in him. William James says that about the saints. It applies. The same applies to what we call in religious terms sinners. Take the sexual impulse at the heart of everything. In some it's weak, in others strong, and everybody has to let it out to keep his life balanced. But in some the impulse is so strong that the emotions and the mind are directed toward sex every minute of the time; and even when it seems they are handling something else, they are totally directed toward that end, they are thinking it every minute and when the moment comes which most of us can skirt even if we'd like to commit an act at that instant *he* can't skirt it, won't skirt it—because he can't face *not* doing it, cannot face what we call civilization. He breaks down before civilization—he *reverts*, yes, it's that: At that moment he reverts, and perhaps not only for that moment. He's an animal. He's a pit bull or Doberman pinscher. He's no different. But if you suggest reversion, people are as insulted as if Darwin had said they were related to apes or dragged into the famous monkey trial on evolution. Shusman never said a word, but he never took his eyes off my brother. Maybe my brother hit him right between the eyes. Maybe he was afraid of him. Maybe he thought of nothing else after that because what my brother said was too true and threw up some kind of obstacle, and maybe my brother in Shusman's mind actually became the obstacle. Maybe he thought my brother was so close to the truth that he suspected him and had to get rid of him before he made some kind of connection and hit on the truth. That was Mark's work. He would have done wonderful things with his research, his dissertation, what would've come of it . . . I've thought and thought. It took me forever to come round to that, what your son said that night, *I've got a one-track mind*, as if I were struggling to see some little thing that might mean—maybe I was looking too deep, but it came like a little thing deep underwater that finally surfaced. And . . . I may be absolutely wrong . . . may be building from nothing . . . but what else? What reason can I find to explain why he killed my brother, why anybody would . . .?

To be truthful, Tom, when I saw him on the beach by the boulders, I wasn't afraid for my life, though I had no idea at all who he was; but I *was* apprehensive—because of the way he appeared and kept coming back and not advancing beyond some point he seemed to have fixed for himself. And listening to him since, I still have that feeling—because he seems to keep fixing that point farther ahead as he approaches it.

My brother finished his work, a draft of his dissertation. I had all his papers, boxes of stuff, metal files filled with notes on cards; a file, three drawers, of case studies. I talked to his advisor several times. Mark's book is brilliant, he said, his theory of human reversion logically worked out and more than substantiated. He said what my brother had said: There are immense prejudices to overcome. How do you suggest that human beings do what dogs do, revert? or that without serious thought given to relieving people of their repressions from early years on we may have more cases of reversion than we'd ever dreamed of? Mark knew one of the key social problems was people's refusing to recognize they share the criminal's makeup, if in different degree. We refuse, Mark said, to recognize what we are. We have too many social fears and we must revise them. Mark always used to say, though he didn't care for crowds, Think what the masses might turn to if they didn't get instant relief from rock concerts, sports, any mass public gathering that avoids a negative accumulation of repressions which can, and not so slowly, turn a whole nation into a herd as Hitler and others have done—that's the mass equivalent to what happened to Randolph Shusman the individual. Anyway, Professor Mann believes he can get a publisher to do the book. I turned everything over to him. It's all I could do for Mark.

Tom, I can't stop dreaming. For some time, except off and on, I hadn't had any nightmares. It's the boy, of course. *He* can't help it, but he's stirred the silt. Days I'm fine, serene, but nights my mind dredges up horrors, they're not happening to *me*, I seem to be looking through a window, it all happens there, I see it so clearly, everything in me wants to scream, stop him, help him, but I can't move, I can't do a thing, and then I realize somebody's holding me there to watch, somebody's pressing my face against the window, I can't turn my head to see who it is.

Do you remember what you dreamed?

Parts that repeat themselves, but some must be too terrible to remember, my mind seems to wipe them out at once, I can't recall them . . . but in the worst there's always that face I can't see.

Your mind's protecting you.

I don't know. . . . I think—I feel certain—if I could see the face, the nightmares would stop. If I could only prolong the dream long enough or wake myself and then will myself back into it and change what happens . . . I understand some people can do that.

If you could, you *would* have—you want to badly enough—but I'm convinced that only time or maybe some radical change in your life may rid you of the nightmares.

Another! That's the last thing I want.

Or anybody'd want for you—unless it's positive.

You mean the nightmares will take care of themselves?

I mean the body's miraculous. I mean just don't give up people. We're the cure. You come to supper tonight.

You!

You're doing it again.

What?

Laughing.

She laughed.

My brother claimed: In a way every criminal is a scapegoat for our crimes except that he does the deed. Every criminal takes his own crimes on his shoulders without asking us. Jesus took our sins on his shoulders without asking us. According to legend, he too presumed. For that presumption he was made a scapegoat. But his impulse was to save, not destroy. He had his kingdom within him. He wanted his father. He had to die for that. He had to be killed or his death would have been as insignificant as ours. There was no other way. He wanted to live *here*, but he wanted—and wanted us—to live forever. His vision demanded his death as faith. To live he had to die. He answered what was inside him. Randolph

Shusmann answered what was inside him too. Did he want to die too? Were they answering the same irrational impulse—to *know* what it is, to invite their own death, to die *into* it or be killed *into* it? Is it all the same thing? Did Randolph Shusmann answer his subliminal impulse to tempt himself to his own death, to go into that *other terrain* he could never know unless he killed? Why is Judas so terrible to us? Because *his* crime included all crimes. Because we're Judas. Every little crime is a glimmer of his enormous crime. By betraying Jesus, he assumed in his own crime all the sins Jesus took on his shoulders; and that was the most heinous crime in all history because he killed with the word. But Judas was also responsible for saving all men by that "murder." If Judas had not done a criminal deed, how would Jesus' life have served mankind? The terror is that every murder serves mankind in one way or another. Every crime is a revelation. Every crime is a reminder of what we are. We hate Judas because we hate that reminder. Every crime is a warning either to know what we are or to become imbalanced and destroy and *through that destruction* be reminded of what we are. Didn't Jesus know that? Didn't Jesus know he needed Judas? That was his major recognition. In Judas he recognized part of himself, or not for one moment could Jesus have been a man or a martyr. He owes it to Judas, perverse debt that that is.

Tom, I could almost believe something had sent that boy, Ralph, to make me face the nightmares. I suppose I'm like most parents, thinking I must have done something wrong or Ran wouldn't have turned out that way and whatever I did wouldn't have turned on me. If only—

You know better than that.

Yes. But it's hard *not* to think that way.

Nonetheless, there's no connection. You couldn't change the genes or anything else.

But that doesn't mean I'm not responsible.

Up to that point we all are because we're here—and breed.

Exactly.

Listen, Minna, as far as we're all one thing, perhaps; but you *know* that's no cause for personal guilt—compassion, yes, but guilt's something else.

But it's assuming responsibility that's important.

Yes, but *how* you assume it is everything, and there's no design for that.

Oh, if only there were!

After it happens, we look back and convince ourselves we've seen a design in it.

I don't know, Tom. Since it hasn't happened yet . . . .

On a Saturday afternoon from the kitchen window she saw someone meandering through the woods. She had no doubt who it was. Ralph Ridley. He was small and sturdy. Ran was. She shuddered but could not take her eyes off him as he approached. She was never sure now, as she wasn't when she looked down to spot him by the boulders. But he *was* real. She was no longer startled. She had come to expect him as part of the configuration of the beach. Presently he appeared, but this time he did not keep his distance—he came straight up the drive to the back door.

She was at the door before he knocked.

He was smiling. A great day for walking, he said.

And the day was—bright, crisp November, a whipping wind off the waves.

For an instant they stood staring at each other before she said Who could get tired of walking the beach?

But he had never approached the beach from her property.

He stood there.

Curious, she dared.

Will you come in for some coffee?

It *would* hit the spot. He smiled.

Inside, when she led him into the living room with a bold view of the beach, he said There's so much light in here it's like being outside.

We—Josh and I—designed it that way. We both hated dark houses. I never liked feeling enclosed.

Does anybody?

I don't know. Some love tiny nooks.

I suppose. Me, I love space. I could stand and watch the waves all day.

They're mesmerizing, yes. Waves remind me of grief, and then peace—how they come again and again and never cease coming—and how your own grief doesn't matter except to you, and how ultimately perhaps no grief matters. The boulders have seen it all, and they're still here. When I was a child I used to pick a wave and say That's mine and watch it come closer and closer and then suddenly strike the shore and turn to foam and be sucked back into the waves.

She fell silent. Out there was sea, sky, space . . . infinite. You dreamed *free*, felt saw smelled ate breathed *freedom*. It was hard then to convince yourself of Ran's cell. Or grave. *Tom, I've* been *with Ran in the prison, but I can't* imagine *Ran there* now. *Something's happening to me. When I remember, when I see the photos in the papers, I think I'm in somebody else's head.* But moments when the sight erupted on the waves, sand, blue sky, it choked breath, she closed her eyes but Ran in his cell stayed stark clear under her lids. And suddenly nothing. *Lethal.* You knew *something* could take freedom. Thought could take it from you too. You went timeless. You entered the darkness you carry and are forever standing in. Then no space gave freedom.

Now she said to Ralph You usually walk the beach. Why'd you come this way today?

He was sitting against the falling sun, stark, his hair lit, but his face dark. She moved so the sun wouldn't blind—he had to turn to her—and she could see his face clear.

I wanted to feel what it was like to walk up the path, home.

Home?

Like him.

But you couldn't—

No.

But what, she wondered, was the difference, *the* if she could know it difference, the *the*, between them? She could go mad, she could go mad all her life thinking such thoughts. The terrible difference, she thought, is he's here, Ran's not.

But why did you try? I mean, why do you want to?

I'm not sure. How can I be sure? I might find out something—

Why would you think you'd find out *anything* when it's all done, over, facts are facts, there aren't any more facts to find out—

Facts? I don't care for facts.

You said *find out*—

About you, about myself maybe—because I had to tell somebody about how I remembered that meeting with your . . . with Randolph.

You couldn't have gone to his lawyer?

And what good would that have done so long after the execution but give them a theoretical reason why your son killed Mark? Just for the record?

To clear your brother's name?

The autopsy did that. There was no suggestion of anything like sexual foul play.

Then?

Then *me*.

You?

Maybe I simply had to *say* what I felt had happened, at least what I knew that had never been said at any time to anybody else. To confess, maybe.

Confess?

Because *I* introduced them. And who could I confess to—a priest? God? I could shout it at the top of my lungs to the waves, couldn't I? But what good would that do? It had to be some*body* and somebody who would understand and care. You lost your son, I lost my brother. Who else but you? So I could bring you what I know, what I have—

The voice startled. His face was suddenly wrenched with agony. Sometimes in stillness, groping for understanding, she felt her face must be distorted like that.

You felt you had . . . She did not want to say *that right*. You had to come?

Yes.

And that it was . . . fair to me.

Fair to you?

You never thought what it might do to me?

Do?

He looked blunted, then a rather wondering look came over his face, he glanced down.

I should have thought. I never meant—don't mean—to hurt you. It never struck me you wouldn't want to know everything I could . . . bring you.

Oh, I do, though . . . I don't know that I'd have wanted to if you'd called or written that you had something to tell me about Ran, and even if I'd said no, something in me, I know, would have wanted to know the least thing, anything, about him.

I was sure hearing it would help you because just telling it would help me. That was selfish. I see that now.

Except that you're right. Talking does help, though it costs—it dredges everything up, and maybe that's not the worst thing because you could rot with it, couldn't you?

He was staring.

Couldn't you? she repeated.

She saw he was studying her, he never took his eyes off her, dared not blink. He was drawing her in, everything. How he must need . . . What he must need . . . . Perhaps because even now she was too saturated with the murders, the trial, all the tensions, and Ran's execution, something in her warned— He's so obsessed. And she saw *him*, Ran, his face with that look she had never in her life associated with him, his fixed features, silence, the *undeviating* stare, *undeviating*. Ran. Mine. What you don't know. Can't. Is it possible? How can you not know your own son, your own blood?

How does it feel to be the mother of . . .?

Rot, he said. Yes, I could. It was happening to me, my mind, in Rockford. I had to clear it. It's better now.

Then it has been worth it.

But you? I did want to help you too, give you some relief. I will.

By telling me your brother and his ideas? and trying to find *reasons* for Ran's doing what he did? *That* doesn't explain all those girls . . . .

She turned, rose, went to the window. How many times she'd seen it all down there! She had looked down on that sea so often to escape, and sometimes she did, she did, but then . . . so often . . . it was all down there too, clear, she could see it, it would come . . . .

How does it feel . . .

You'll have to excuse me. There are things I must do. Perhaps . . . another day.

I could come?

If it helps you . . . Yes.

And you?

Me?

Does it help you?

She was silent. She studied his face. She had kept expecting him, even imagining him. He had become familiar.

Well, it will, he said, I know it will. I have something I wanted you to . . . but not today, when the time's right . . . .

Alerted, she raised her hand almost to touch him, to keep him from leaving, but said When the time's right, yes. Goodbye.

So long, he said.

But watching him—he took the path down to the sand—she was filled with curiosity, and apprehension.

Tom said: Brig tells me the boy's working out fine on the job. They all like him. I didn't say a thing about who he was; I didn't want to be unfair and spoil his chances if there's no reason to.

Beyond Tom and Sue's dining room window the Widow's Hole glowed with morning sun, the piers dark streaks in the water, the boats barely rocking in the vague heave, the hospital reflected deep in the water. In this Sunday quiet she felt that momentary displacement, as if she were really inverted.

He's been to the house twice now. He's got something on his

mind, he's hesitant to say what it is—he said he's waiting for the right moment.

And you're sure you're not afraid? Sue said. She set the pot roast, oven-brown potatoes, carrots, onions—beautiful—on the table and sat. She was a miracle of order, and after church to boot.

Apprehensive maybe, but afraid? Not really. Actually the boy inspires confidence, he's so sincere. Oh, I know, Tom, the worst are sometimes the best actors, under innocent faces . . . and he does have one, and he has every reason to be—what?—angry, vengeful, unforgiving—but if he's any of that, I've been taken in completely by his . . . devotion to his brother, some desire he really has to orient himself—and sometimes, I feel, me. And there are moments . . . He has dark hair and green eyes and long lashes and very full lips and a rather far look sometimes, and he's small . . . and when he's sitting there talking to me . . . in that chair . . . .

She looked out over the Widow's Hole, past the bay and Shelter Island, where it was all far, far sky.

In the silence she knew they too were seeing Ran sitting in that chair.

But, Tom said—his hand covered hers—You have to remember he's not.

I remember—every second, she said.

It was Sue who said, But it must sometimes be pleasant to confuse them.

She smiled. Yes, *yes*, of course! Sue, always placid, the serene blue eyes in a face made austere, and more beautiful, by blonde hair drawn taut in a bun and accenting her fine bones. Sue, in her understanding and always in that soft, so peaceful voice, verbalized what she herself hadn't quite realized until it *was* said.

Though, Minna said, when you're so close to it, you don't always see . . . And then it occurred to her: You two don't want to meet him?

It *was* in the back of my mind, Tom said.

It might . . ., she said. *Might what?* she thought. Force his hand? Place him? Finally bring out—what? End it?

In silence they waited.

I don't know what it might do, she said.

Ralph did not take to the meeting.

Oh, he was the boy next door, Sue said, having been captivated by his intimate smile, his eyes, his look of boyish innocence. He's the kind you want to put your arm around and assure.

You say so because he wouldn't talk, Tom said.

Why, he talked a blue streak, Sue said. What you mean is he shied away from any talk about his brother, what you wanted to pin him down to, Sue said. But he certainly went on about the island, town, his parents, Rockford, Chicago, the university—actually for all his apparent naïveté he's certainly very social.

Tom, Minna said, I told you I didn't know what it might do. Quite simply, it made him go silent.

Why, do you suppose? Tom said.

I'd say because you were treading on sacred ground, Minna said.

His brother?

And my son. I think he was telling you both it's private, ours. It's between us. His silence is a message to stay out of it. He's jealous, in short.

Jealous.

He's guarding jealously what's his—for me.

And he's right to, Sue said. It binds you two. To him we have no business there. We're nothing to him.

We are to her, Tom said.

Yes, but *he* doesn't know that, and if he did . . . we're still not Minna and Ralph, are we?

I'm not so sure, Tom said.

I knew you'd say that, Minna said. What did we ever do to deserve this man, Sue?

Ralph would sit on the rocks below. He looked as if he belonged there. When he was not there, she imagined, as so often over the years, how strange the landscape must have been eons before. And how often she had imagined the first time strange fish creatures had leaped into the air, the first time maybe something outside of the sea had entered their eyes and tugged at something in them, drawn them, made something in them yearn for that view; or the air they had drawn in made such new pain pleasure it had teased *do* and *do* and *do* and stirred lungs, lungs had desired air, had had to have air. More and more she imagined, saw, how the first strange creatures had flopped the first time up onto that beach and eons after had become . . . this, us, me, Ran.

Oh, Ran, she murmured, Ran.

She stared down at that boy on the rock rising and falling in her tears. OhmyGod, Ran, Ran.

In that instant Ran cried out to her. She could have run to the bedroom to answer that cry from the cradle, that cry which tore his whole life over her eyes, his life in this house, on the beach, in town, at school, moments when he was picked on, fought, the day he nearly drowned, his broken leg in a fall from the highbar at gym, his thick dark wavy hair, the lips too red and always wet, his brown dark dark eyes in which you could see nothing but yourself, the sight of him playing in the woods, down there on the beach, Ran, Ran—and some moments she was sure that that other, that nightmare, had never been and he *was* down there, Ran was walking the beach, he was sitting on a boulder, she could rush out onto the sundeck and wave and shout Ran Ran Ran, and at moments she was so sure, so sure, that she did move, slid the door aside and rushed out and halted at the rail, startled at herself, sobered, and cried out to herself You fool, you! You knew it was that boy. You knew it. What's happening to you?

Ralph told her: What you have to know is that among inmates anything is possible in prison. Professor Mann says One-to-one criminals are much smarter than any guard; it always takes many minds to master the one criminal. He says it's always been the case. Evil by itself is powerful. Good is weak. To be strong, the good have to band together. It takes any number of good people to overcome one evil person—well, you've seen that a thousand times—and chances are any number of the good may be destroyed in the process. The one-to-one combat—one cop, one crook—we used to read about is almost impossible except in the movies. It always represented the ideal; the hero was a savior, rare, and he saved men from their own cowardice. He was a model. Professor Mann's no fool. My brother worked under him. Professor Mann had every faith in Mark. He saw Mark's genius—yes, *he* called Mark that, it's not my word. How would I have had any idea he was a genius. He was just my brilliant brother. Anyway, before Mark was executed, Professor Mann tried to interview him on Death Row—he had tried Ran's lawyer and his psychiatrist, but the prison authorities refused all such contact with him, despite Professor Mann's argument that an interview might be of infinite value in helping to avoid such crimes in the future by advancing an understanding of ourselves which we have never brought to people before they gave way to madness.

It was a curious coincidence. That prison had been the richest source of Mark's research. There was a guard. Time and again Mark had gone to the prison during this guard's shift and the guard knew what Mark was working on. Obviously he respected that, so—this is the coincidence—when Professor Mann pursued it, he came across the guard who knew what Mark was working on. As everyone knows, there's always that tit-for-tat understanding among guards and prisoners and prisoners and prisoners—information, job shifts, easing up on rec time, holding their tongue, whatever; and the guard was not above betting what he wanted on the sly. So one day when Professor Mann was on his way out, the guard said If Shusman'll talk–no promises because Shusman just says what he has to—tell me what you're after, there are ways to goad. And the guard—no name, Professor Mann promised that–came through. He must have been a hawk, that guard, or whoever on the same row caught it—

Caught?

On tape.

Tape! she said. *Tape?*

Yes.

Ran—on tape? But why didn't you—

Tell you right away?

Yes!

Don't you know what, out of the blue, that would have done to you? . . . Don't you?

I'm afraid so.

And *I* was afraid. Am. But—

Please don't put it off. Now—this afternoon—after work. Can you? If I have to anticipate it all night, I . . . you can't imagine what it will be like.

Can't imagine . . . She heard his hesitation.

I'm sorry. I shouldn't have said that. It was thoughtless of me. Come early and I'll give you some supper.

As soon as I can clean myself up after work.

Yes. Then.

But all afternoon she was in agony, *Ran, Ran*, though half saved thank God by her impulse to ask Ralph to supper—she had to get it ready, try to keep part of her mind at least on that, but thinking, no, not so much thinking as erupting Ran in bits flashes scenes, a chaos that stopped, came, flowed, broke. So that when the knock came it thundered everything still, blank, for an instant.

Oh, I'm so relieved you're here, she said. The afternoon's been, frankly, hell.

I maybe shouldn't have told you all that. His voice was tender. I've put it off, I've been afraid to tell you, maybe I shouldn't have, I'd even thought of destroying the tape.

No!

It's a copy. Professor Mann has the original.

Afraid, she had to follow her fear, face it, rid herself of it.

Now that you've told me about it, I have to hear it, she said. I'd always wonder—I've been wondering—what you kept from me. I'd hold it against you. But I'm glad you're here. I don't think I could stand to hear it alone.

But thinking *Not yet*. No. *Anything* to postpone fulfill her fear desire, avoid. She said, Supper's ready. Let's eat first.

Out the kitchen window the woods were dark now, only the

tips of the naked trees edged with dying light. He, his presence, eased her.

You're an ace of a cook. I love lasagna.

Most men I know do. My friend Tom pesters me for it.

He should. It's worth it.

She laughed. But he's a friend. He and Sue spoil me. They've been my salvation.

You're lucky. Not everybody has friends who can save them.

His soft voice was such a lament and his gaze so still on the plate that she reached over and touched his hand.

For a long moment he stared at her hand, for it continued to rest there. She could say nothing—by touching his hand she had startled herself. *When, how long since . . .* Ran. *The mother of.* Josh. *Her Jew.* Oh, she *knew* town. But they had never touched or been touched by him. Josh. And Ran. Hers. And forever.

For a little after coffee they sat. Dark had absorbed the woods and they could see only themselves in the panes.

She rose abruptly.

Let's have some light, she said. And went into the living room. It was suddenly too big, and empty. Come, she said.

And said, Go ahead.

And waited.

It's very short. He sat in the Fireside Josh and then Ran had loved.

She closed her eyes.

She heard the cassette player click. Her temples throbbed.

There came an instant's fuzziness and then the voice. At the first word her blood head cried silently *Ran it can't be it's Ran.* She caught her breath with her hands, gasped through her fingers, and did not could not move, frozen by his voice:

. . . *you*, you think I got no balls, and *you*? you sniped four on the freeway because you didn't have the guts to put a hand on them. That's balls? And never saw them shake their little asses at you so I have to go for them, think night day I'll shove it so far up their cunt they'll choke to death on my come and when I'm through they'll eat my cock their own blood and cock stuffed in their mouths up them so nobody else, no, nobody'll ever have them, they're mine, mine, and hacked so nobody, *nobody* else—yes, mine buried for me where only I . . . *You*, you son-of-a-bitch, Harrels, what is this? What're you up to, you goddamn motherfucker? . . .

Ralph clicked it off.

There was a long silence and then she moaned, she stood up, she stood there. Ran, she cried out, swaying, moaning, Ran Ran Ran, and broke, sank back down into the chair in great heaves and cries.

In an instant he was beside her, he clutched her face between his hands and drew it to him, his hands went around her shoulders. She let herself fall against him, her breath heaving in convulsive chokes and she cried, trying to talk, . . . Ran . . . never . . . death . . . who . . . killed . . ., until she saw or felt or knew he was crying too, and she put her arms around him, embraced, Poor boy, thinking his *brother*, both crying, and for a long time they held each other till the crying ceased and the stillness itself in the room became a presence.

Finally, Ralph separated himself, slid back on his haunches.

I knew it would be hard, but I knew you'd want to hear it no matter what.

She nodded, but she was half not in the room, she was half *not*. In this stillness she was somewhere raging, raging . . . and how could she be? She stared at him. She said, I feel . . . my body feels . . . stark raving mad. I think . . . Again she rose abruptly. She stood there an instant. She let out a great cry and covered her mouth with both hands. I could die, die, she said. I'm going to lie down. My bedroom—

If she could make it.

Me. Let *me*. He supported her to her room.

So it's this, she thought. She sat on the bed. *I'm about to collapse.*

I'll stay. I'll be right here—in the living room on the couch. You call if you need me, anything . . . . He drew down the spread for her and the sheets. There . . . .

She cannot move. One hand clutches her neck, the other from behind presses her face against the window. Each time she goes to scream the hand cuts her breath off. She tries to close her eyes, but the lids freeze. She cannot even blink. She can see the girl, and streets houses the house the door the room, but she moves, is moving with him, in him, she's doing what he's doing, can't choose not to do what he's doing as he does it, touches, kisses, violates, strips, and strikes stabs kills, the blood spurts over her hands, face, clothes, he mutilates and bags and she must go to the woods and dig, digs, buries. She cannot stop doing, and she sees him again, the girls, the streets . . . and again, again—she must stop, stop being him, stop him, stop seeing—must—and with all her will wrenches, wrenches her head, and screams and wrenches her head, breaks free of sex blood bodies and turns to discover that face Who? *and stares, she is staring at that face* You! *and can't believe No* no *and tries to close her eyes but can't close out what she won't believe but knows* Ran, *Ran's face, Ran, it's you.*

You mean, Tom said, the boy wouldn't go, Minna?

I mean Ralph wouldn't leave me in the house by myself as distraught as I was by Ran's voice on the tape. Oh, Tom, it was so . . . I don't know . . . there's no word for what Ran said, but I *wanted* the sound of him, I wanted him to stop *talking* but didn't want his sound to stop . . . I felt he was in the room, but I didn't *know* him from what he said. I could *see* what he said, the same horrors I couldn't shut out of my nightmares. I kept thinking It can't be my Ran, but it *was*, it *was* his voice, it was my Ran I knew but didn't know, and don't know now, and never will. I, at least the moment when it was over, couldn't confront it. Ralph was wonderful. He slept on the couch all night, got up early and walked all that way to work—I didn't hear a thing, I was so out of it—leaving a note that he'd be by when he got off work, to see if I was all right.

But did Ralph *have* to play you the tape?

Oh, yes—but as much for himself as for me. He said he knew I'd want the voice. The more he thought, he said, he knew what it might do to me and was even afraid, why he'd kept putting it off, but, he said, I'd know then—somehow Ran might be put in his place in my head forever—and in *his* too, Ralph's, because he had to be with me when I heard it, he insisted to himself on that, on being with me, the only other person it could possibly matter to. In a way it would end the *worst part* of it for both of us: We'd be left with no choice but to accept together what Ran had done to his life and his victims' and our lives, and *how*, though maybe never in this world why. And face to face we'd confront that truth together and be left with . . . that silence . . . what else could there be? . . . and—oh, he's no fool, that boy—he knew that vacuum bound us even when we were half the country apart though we didn't know each other except for almost forgotten photos in the newspapers; and now some understanding binds us and a compassion we didn't even have to speak but that came. Oh, no, he's no fool. Somehow, blind he knew, his instinct told him to follow his feelings. He came straight to the only person he could help. What he really didn't know was how it would help him. We're the only two in the world . . . well, we've seen it together. And . . . I'm so glad he came, Tom.

So am I—now. I hate to say how wrong I was. I'd have said—

Don't. Rest your case. She laughed.

I'm glad yours is rested, though you know you're bound to have momentary relapses.

Oh, I don't forget that. But I'm prepared—no, fortified—for that.

Thanks to Ralph.

Now you sound more like Sue than yourself!

Haven't I good reason?

You! You always turn it back on me.

That's a lawyer's tactic.

Winter days after work were dark so Ralph walked the shore weekends, sometimes sheltering himself from the blow behind the great boulders and then coming on, down past the house and round the point toward East Marion. Now she expected the small figure in the mackinaw with the matching cap and black gloves.

The days he missed she felt bereft. Afternoons when she was home, on his return she'd flag him up for coffee, a drink, snack, supper; but when he missed two weekends in a row, she became restless. She called Brig at the lumber company: Ralph was out with a bronchial cold, came back to work, came down with pneumonia and is in the hospital.

Hospital!

Yes, but they're letting him out tomorrow.

Oh, Brig, thanks—

She called the hospital. When are you discharging Ralph Ridley?

Doctor Spurling will check him at eleven. He'll probably dismiss him then.

In the morning she waited until Doctor Spurling left and Ralph appeared.

But—what's wrong! he said.

You're what's wrong. She took his arm. Did you intend to walk home. It may be a small town, but it's also winter and if I know anything you're unsteady on your pins.

Oh, lady, you've got that right!

She laughed. Hang on, then.

As she was driving along the North Road, he said You always take the long way home?

Cheer up! One way or another you'll get home.

But she turned up her drive.

You haven't got time—

Hush. You've got to have a good lunch, she said.

Parked, she said, Now just sit tight. I'll help you out. You're not so strong as you think.

Inside, he sat in the living room, trying not to breathe so hard.

Let go, she said. You have nothing to hide here.

When you catch your breath, you go in that room, take your clothes off and get into bed, and when it's ready, I'll bring you some lunch.

But I've got to get to my own room.

What would you do at the Manaton House anyway?

He turned his face up to her, raised his hand, but quick she moved away.

It was only later when she heard him cross the living room that she turned from her work and saw him standing in the doorway to Ran's room, so hauntingly small, so familiar, that in her momentary confusion twenty years vanished and she trembled and almost dropped the casserole before she recalled who he was.

THE WINTER GUEST

Snow came, and winds bitter and as relentless as a curse over town. But the regulars and die-hards—insatiate of talk, cards, the camaraderie of drink—bucked the blow to reach the club hunched into the slope of the crick like a disreputable thing jealous of its privacy. Even in good weather The Triangle is not visible from the street and the few high houses that line the bank along this narrow finger of the harbor. The crick is a dead end with a surface usually so still that it barely stirs the beer and Coke cans, the paper cups, tissues, corks, condoms and the oil that floats shimmering and serpentine around the boats moored at the piers standing on spidery legs. The club's picture window makes a great eye, blank yet vigilant over shallows of deep sea grass to the road that runs past the Protestant and Catholic cemeteries, those islands of stones propped against oblivion, and past a stretch of field through the woods, and opens abruptly on the sea and Shelter Island and infinite sky.

The snow ceased suddenly, settled, and the view returned, a world frozen and silent and ghostly waiting for the sun to burn to the quick, turn the innocent snow to slush, and bare the dark beneath.

Surely that day everyone in The Triangle or the Stirlington hotel or the Wyandank, everyone in Helen's bar or Frank's or the Legion hall, perhaps everyone in town, was remembering—could not help remembering:

Because he came in winter, this brother to the mayor. What

wind brought him, this traveler? And if Devon the mayor put his brother, Randy, up for a weekend, the following Monday he was rooming at the Manaton House on First, and then seen in the driver's seat of one of his brother's lumber trucks and most days afterward at The Diner or Cozy Corner, easing into conversation, good talker that he was, the younger brother, and good-looker, with the black hair curly and thick that, you could see, drew women's eyes and made their fingers quiver. Soon so familiar and everywhere, with his flash of very white teeth and laughing eyes, but most the voice insinuating with invisible tentacles, he became as welcome as a spark on the coldest day or darkest night (There's Randy), as expected as the dawn (Here he comes).

But this is not Randy Tidwell's story, for he does not count here, Carmela; and it is not his brother's story or his brother's wife's, Martha's; and not your son Brand's, though he is at the core of it. It is, finally, your story, Carmela, though you hardly appear in it, because you were the source of the fourteen years lowered into the ground on Tuesday. When you uttered that one whimper at the grave, who could not share your grief? Surely that whimper contained all the joy of penetration and orgasm and generation and the slow shifting of your body's functions and its discomforts and distortion; the separation of your own self from inside you in that tiny viscid creature the instant the cut cord severed him and the cry slapped into him was your own cry and all our cries repeated; and then the milk and suck and the warm mesmeric flow; and in him too your man dead and the boy only six, and the years of living on a public pittance and housecleaning, years you walked him to school and back before and after each day's cleaning. What father's son was he? Who knew, knows? You were the silent public declaration that a woman's body may be used and used by many men and one man still desire and love and forgive and take her in as Dennis Bascomb took you in, brought you home from the city with your hands holding your swollen belly and you with your eyes closed surely feeling that life beating gently, insistently, even under your lids.

I cannot rescue your son, Carmela, from the oblivion that

will be my own one day. I write this story for him, who will never read it, and for you, who will never know, Carmela, and surely for me—to unravel, understand, believe. For words are the last stand against oblivion. We must talk our lives into some imagined order that does not exist.

Because before Dennis Bascomb brought you home, Carmela, he and old Tom had been lifelong friends, and no day that Dennis went to The Triangle did he fail to stop by my grandfather Tom's, a few houses from the crick. So it was natural that when your Brand was born Tom came to feel like the boy's second father, and over the years became that. After Dennis had died, anybody might see Tom and Brand after school, fishing off the railroad dock or as far off as Pete Neck or Orient or netting crabs in the shallows or sometimes pulling up lobster pots dropped and staked in the Sound. But Tom was too wise to let the boy neglect his talents since he knew too well what the prison of *poor* and *ignorant* could lead to in this town at the end of the world with few jobs, boredom, drink, *down* and *out*, welfare. Tom told you The teacher said Brand has music in his fingers, he's got to use them. Tom told me you laughed with pleasure, Carmela, but did not realize. But Tom did. He saw—how he saw!—in a waking dream he saw Brand playing the piano, Brand one day playing in Carnegie Hall, on television . . . . It was in that way that Brand's lessons with Martha began the year before Randy came, gratis you thought, but given by old Tom the father, who in his peripheral manner—occasionally running into Martha at the A&P or passing the Tidwell house on Front Street and stopping an instant to catch the sound—was casually vigilant.

And it was Brand, stopping at Tom's for a bite after his lesson, who told Tom Now there's the brother. Tom said What brother? Devon's, he said. Mr. Tidwell's, Tom said, you're too young to be calling him Devon. Yes, Mr. Tidwell then, *his* brother, he's come to live here. He came in the middle of my lesson so Mrs. Tidwell let me go. He—Randy's his name—shook my hand. I thought he'd break it. Tom smiled but said Let's see it. Can't have anything happening to those hands.

It was the first Tom heard of the younger brother's coming back, though he knew Devon had a younger brother. He remembered the blight on the family name—old in town—when his mother ran off with a younger man and took the younger son and left with the father.

Old Tidwell, a long time ill, had died a year and more ago, but no second son had shown at his funeral.

In no time and frequently, in my own drop-ins at The Triangle some evenings and mostly weekends, I would come upon Randy playing cards—good company, the regulars (who seldom let a novice break into their games) said, and good at cards, no drinker and clear-headed. And who wouldn't admire that? His looks and habits and his sudden guileless smile boosted the mayor's image. And soon, with the spring and mobility, Randy was out on this one or that one's boat fishing, or scalloping at Pete Neck, or crabbing in the shallows—trusted by the drinkers, who could always use a level head to keep the boat and the day straight.

So it was natural that Brand, if he went almost as often to Tom's as ever, did not stay as long. Once a week, after the Sunday dinner which Randy was invited to at his brother's, Randy would borrow his brother's boat; and he and Brand would come home with a mess of porgies or bass or weakfish or on some days crabs, and Brand always with a blow-by-blow story of their day to tell Tom. And before Tom could ask, Brand would say, No, nothing happened to my hands, making Tom laugh and take the cat Shasta onto his lap, and stroke her, satisfied.

It happened in spring with the increased work in construction that Randy chose as his helper a man known to be short on brains but a worker, half brute, who could toss lumber like straw. It was evident, and shortly, how doglike Willis took to Randy; and it was the source of jokes among the workers at the yard that Willis Akens was as much animal as man—you had only to glance at that hulk. In the water he could lie on his back and spout like a whale. And after a while, it was common to see that unlikeliest three—Randy, Brand, and Willis—weekends or after work all through the summer fishing or swimming or roaming the docks, watching the Fourth of July parade, enjoying the carnivals or the firemen's fair or the bazaar at St. Mary's Church, and so on to Labor Day and back-to-school time for Brand, and through the waning fall.

Martha all the year had exacted Brand's lessons to the minute, and more, and as always before with her private pupils, to give them presence and pride in hard work, she announced a recital in her living room to allow Brand to show his year's achievement. She invited first his mother, then those who loved music and teaching, and let Brand invite a few friends. That explained why on that day, among Martha's little elite, figured—besides her brother-in-law, Randy—not only Brand's puppy love Nessa and his school friend Jon, but his fishing mate Willis, a self-conscious hunch in the odd clothes Randy must have forced him into wearing.

It was Willis who was carried away by what sounds Brand's fingers could make. He talked of nothing afterward but the rich perfume of the music and how soft and beautiful music was, soft to make your eyes close blind and still see it and almost touch it. His fingers quivered when he told it. Yes, Randy said, that's how it is, only there's a lot more to it, Willis. No doubt, to Randy it had come time—we at The Triangle and people everywhere in town would later pinpoint the recital, decide that that was the crucial moment, though true beginnings are too far back ever to trace, the moment that propelled Randy toward his departure. And it was a tribute to Randy's temperament that once he had chosen, he had the discipline to direct all his energies to his very special purpose, which no Martha and no Devon—though they had every reason not to be deceived—was made aware of. And it was the talk too of the lumberyard that Willis Aken had developed an obsession, Willis, who never ceased to marvel at Brand's fingers—he would actually look and look and sometimes touch them a light caress. No telling then what he was seeing, though Randy must have known. Nobody understood Willis like Randy. No one took time to. And more and more—through fall toward the inevitable winter—Willis clung to Randy. He must have felt Randy was his salvation, Tom said.

Willis's parents, it seemed, could not be grateful enough to Randy for such a tie. And Devon and Martha marveled at how comfortably Randy had situated himself in town, both comfortable with the sight of the two, Randy as always at Sunday dinner and now Willis appearing outside with metronomic regularity not long after dessert, a familiar around the house, at the gate, and very frequently your boy, Carmela, as if the addition of his trusting face lent credence to the union of that trio, made it perfectly acceptable and unquestioned.

So winter came, and who could have been surprised when Devon let Willis Aken go—after all, in winter construction falls off—and Willis, idle, with his one-track mind, must have felt half crazy, divorced as he was from Randy. Anyone could see him hanging around the Manaton House at the end of Randy's workday or at The Diner or Cozy Corner at noon and sometimes riding with Randy in the truck till Devon tore into Randy because company insurance no longer included Willis. That left Willis a prowler except on some evenings when he accompanied Randy even to The Triangle, where he would sit in that doglike silence and waiting while the others played cards and talked. And when the snows came Willis's dark hulk stood out more conspicuously against that blank white, trudging his accustomed routes to the yard and restaurants and bars on Front and Third streets. And it was much later, too late, that the men in The Triangle and the women at home or in the stores would comment on how that shadow outside Devon Tidwell's house could not have been waiting so often and at any hour for his friend Randy, and in retrospect that waiting bore its true and sinister aspect.

And, though winter and school and his piano lessons confined Brand, no one, despite Willis's free time, would have thought it unnatural to have seen Willis waiting outside Devon Tidwell's, where anyone could see Martha through the front windows and Brand at the piano. Who could have known if Willis was actually listening or, as he had said to Randy and Brand, seeing the music? And who could have known that that music was in Martha, as the music's perfume was, and its touch?

Martha was Devon's treasure. One summer evening, a Friday, he had seen her get off the Long Island train and board the ferry there at the railroad dock—small and fair and young with a woman's quivery soft fullness. He loved to tell us after how he too had bought a ticket on The Islander just to ride the ten minutes over to Shelter Island and find out which hotel she was vacationing in; and how for days after he had left his assistant with the yard, taken his car over and his bathing trunks and planted himself on the beach where she swam; and how after resisting through the week's vacation and the barrage of long distance calls and letters between upstate and town, she consented to meet him in New York City. Not long after, the schoolteacher could be seen overhauling the house on Front Street. But what most impressed was the music, which halted people out front, the sound always audible on the street and in warm weather pouring out over the harbor. And the fall of that year she was at the school, and her personality and talents admired. She was lovely. The men looked at her with wonder and no shame; the women, except rarely, shared her really disinterested dedication.

It was my grandfather, Tom, who had the habit of meditation for the sermons he once gave as itinerant preacher at the church on Chapel Lane and along the North Fork of Long Island, who later pieced much of the story together and who left me to imagine the rest to give it some kind of order, as each of us must, Carmela, to bear it and make something against what may not be, though Tom would claim an order that needed no help from me. Because the alert, too late, did come—the fait accompli suddenly both suspected and realized—and it came to Tom, perhaps even before it had been consummated. Tom perceived something of the vagrant truth when at the hour of his usual piano lesson Brand knocked on Tom's back entry, startling him, who knew where the boy was supposed to be weekday afternoons at four. I thought you'd be at Martha's, Tom said. And something of an intuition was instantly confirmed when Brand, ushered in to warm himself at the kitchen stove this iciest of days, said, I'm afraid, Tom.

Afraid?

I couldn't find the key. It's gone.

Key?

To the back door. She always leaves it under the straw in Jenny Wren's nest in the basket by the back door. It wasn't there, Tom.

She forgot it.

She never forgets.

Everybody does sometime.

But it's not just that. He was staring at the floor—maybe he wanted to be sure again before he said it, or maybe be was just seeing it for the first time. It's . . . there were footprints in the snow—going in, that's all.

All?

No footprints coming out, I mean. I didn't think of that till after I saw Randy.

Randy! But he's not working?

He wasn't in his truck.

But weekdays he's always—

Yes, but I was so glad he was there. I told him No key. What? he said, and I said No key, and he looked hard and then put his arm around me and said Maybe you'd better go tell my brother he's wanted at home, and he was like smiling, Tom, and why was he? That made it worse. But I went to the yard, his brother was there, and I told him she wasn't home and didn't leave me the key and told him Randy said he's wanted at home. What? he said. Home? he said. But if Martha's not— That's all he said. And quick he went. He looked afraid too, like I made him afraid. And I ran. I'll go to Tom's like always, I said, Tom will know. Brand was holding his wet sleeves over the stove. I'm afraid, Tom.

You settle down now, Tom said, and have some clam chowder, I had it ready for you. There's no real reason to be upset at all yet.

And the instant he said yet, Tom realized he had caught some fear.

And don't tell me you're not hungry, growing boys eat all the time. Take this.

Brand crumbled crackers in his bowl but before he had swallowed several spoonfuls, a knock came. It was Cash the cop. Sorry to bother you, Tom, but— Tom saw Cash was relieved at once to see the boy, though the sight of him made Cash's speech halting. Somebody got into the Tidwells' and— Cash interrupted himself to ask Brand You didn't see anyone, son? No, Brand said, no sir. We ask because we saw your footprints beside the other's, and we'd hoped you'd seen someone . . . , him.

Him? Tom said.

Cash gazed waiting at the boy.

Who? the boy said. He went pale, his lids fluttered, his head tilted as if to fall.

Anybody, Cash said.

No. She didn't answer. She wasn't there. Brand stared hard at Cash. She wasn't! he cried and stood straight up. I want her! Where is she?

Devon found her. The man must have just left.

And Martha? Tom said.

They got her straight to the hospital. She was pretty badly— Cash bent close to Tom, his voice went thin—violated.

That's all I wanted to ask you, Cash said to Brand, but before he could leave, the boy dashed across the kitchen and out the door and entry and was already around the corner when Tom cried into the bleak white emptiness after him, Wait! Wait, Brand!

Tom was certain if he did not race home, he would not be long in coming back, and waited.

The knock came, but when he opened the door, he was not only stunned but frightened.

Carmela!

Who had never been near the house, who in fact almost never left her own except to work or shop. Hardly bundled up, she must have hurried. Come in, he said, you'll catch your death.

Before she could ask, he said He went home. But Tom's doubt made it a question.

He didn't. Cash came there first. I told him *here*, they'd find Brand here.

He *was* here. He ran out—home, I was sure. But maybe to the hospital?

Tom could see the hospital lights, three houses away, from his windows.

No. I stopped there because Cash said Martha was— Nobody can see her, she said.

He loves Martha, Tom said. She's his bible.

Through her worry, at that she smiled. No. You're his bible. But she could do no wrong in his eyes.

Can't.

Yes, can't. She was—is—fine.

You'd better wait here, Carmela. Sit. Brand's maybe gone for Randy—

He's gone. The brother's gone. They can't find him anywhere. Devon, Cash said, is sure he's skipped town. Devon said There are reasons; I should have known. The other, Aken—they found him hiding in the truck, Randy's truck, parked at the lumberyard, the last place he must have thought they'd look because Randy had parked it yesterday on account of the weather it seemed, but it must have been because he was leaving, he must have meant to go.

Who knows what he meant to do?

Who ever knows . . .? she said, turning her head. If Brand comes . . . .

I'll be sure he goes straight to you.

Yes, home. Abruptly she touched him, his shoulder—You're always so good to him, Tom—and abruptly left.

He had time, Tom said, to ponder Randy Tidwell—had to, Tom said, because Carmela's visit and his fear now for the boy had left him half frenzied—and it drove all else out of his mind. With all that he could possibly imagine, the horror was that Randy was gone and had left no actual deed for which they could hold him responsible; had touched his brother's wife and therefore his brother without lifting a finger; had destroyed the image of the mayor's good fortune, of a truly fine woman; and had marked his brother the mayor for life, no matter how recuperable what remained.

And gone free, Tom said.

It's always out there, I said.

No, it's in us, it's part of what we are, it knows us, that's why it can deceive us so successfully. Who knows how far its actions reverberate before it ends.

It never ends, I said.

Oh, yes. It exhausts itself.

No, I said, it just goes on.

It is easy to imagine, Tom said, but hard to prove how day after day Randy must have incited Willis, appealed to his lascivious desires, to the music Willis heard embodied in Martha Tidwell's flesh and that drew him with Randy's every goading word. And to that boy, trusting him as he did, Randy could do no wrong, though now I remember Brand's words, though at the time I was as unaware of what he was revealing as he was: How Willis rows! You should see his face when he's rowing, Tom. It makes me afraid. Ma wouldn't let me go if it was just Willis, but Randy's always along, so it's okay. But Tom knew you, Carmela, who knew men but would not speak *against*. In the terms of Tom's faith, at least, you had fallen, and been lifted up, and would cast no stone. And the proof that nobody trusted Randy so much as Brand is that Brand had blurted out where Martha left him the key on days when she would be late.

So when Brand arrived at four and went around to the back porch and knocked and no one came to the door and he reached under the straw, groped and groped, and found no key, seeing those footsteps but not even thinking yet, already his blood was afraid, it knew *something*. Because Willis was still inside or, Tom said, Randy would not be hanging around on foot and his truck nowhere in sight, waiting to be certain, by seeing Willis leave, that the deed was done. Unknowingly Brand was the last one for sure to see Randy in town. Randy must have planned that by the time of Brand's lesson, the boy would knock and frighten Willis . . . It would be terrible. And it is proof of Randy's nature that he most appealed (and had to know it, he *did* know it) to impressionable innocence and would kill it if he had to. Nothing dies so suddenly as innocence. I don't suppose even that bothers him, wherever he is, for there is an evil which has no conscience and no fear of good.

And it was to The Triangle and with the lightning speed of bad news that from one or the other came whatever threads ran through the story that by dark Randy Tidwell was gone from the Manaton House—his room left, by the way, neat as a pin—and with nothing more than the cloth bag he had come with. He must have boarded the train with no ticket because Swen said Randy never appeared at his ticket window, but Minnie and Paul Roach thought they saw him walking through a coach as the six-o'clock train to New York City pulled out.

Who would think that anyone would tarnish his brother's wife, and who Martha, who never did anything we knew to condemn?

She wouldn't have to, Tom said. Being decent's all that's needed to make others fabricate blame. Something in us revels in another's fall.

How could he—Devon would not name him—have wanted anything so badly? They were Devon's words to Martha in the hospital, but they were the town's now. Anything? Martha said. Nothing, Devon said. *That.* Nothing was what the brother had had all his life. Disinherited of father and brother and town and business. And he took nothing with him; he was interested only in the effects his vengeance would leave behind. To do such a thing Randy Tidwell must have had the lucidity of madness, I said. No, Tom said, because madness has no control over its lucidity, and Randy Tidwell had absolute control of his reason. He had his plan, and his mind was never careless.

If the town was hushed by the madness committed by Willis Aken, nothing could predict the paralysis of the moment of discovering Brand's body.

Brand did not go home. He was not there when Camela returned from Tom's place, and she did not wait—she knew he was not coming home or he would already have been there. She knew her boy. She walked the short blocks from Third to the blue neon POLICE sign on Main and said You've got to find him, something's happened to Brand. And at the police's second visit to Tom, Tom went around the corner and past the four houses to the crick and The Triangle and startled the members by standing silent a second by the tiny bar. Brand's gone, he said. Missing. We've got to find that boy. They would perhaps have shrugged—at a false alarm or unfounded sentimentality—if it had not been Tom Verity whom nobody could fault—he believed what he pronounced. And to a man, unquestioning, they dropped their cards and conversation and left their drinks—Be careful! Tom said—and in an instant he could hear a half dozen motors warming up outside. The bartender put out the lights. I'll go with you, Len, Tom said. Oh no you don't, Tom. I'm dropping you off. You're staying inside. We'll get the news to you as soon as there is any. Tom said, I can walk. You get in, Len said.

Brand could not go far. Town is small, a mile wide between the harbor and the Sound, and a mile or so long between Mill Pond and the cemeteries, though with plenty of woods and shallows, and under the worst of freezes that day.

Tom with his faith—his heart hoping against what his mind could not confirm—waited for whoever's car lights would stop out front to bring him news. But it was not one of the men in The Triangle who came. It was—and despite all his own wretchedness—Devon Tidwell who brought him the news, who almost could not speak, till Tom said It's the boy? Devon nodded, Tom said. Devon could hardly tell it, it took him time. Floating in the crick by the hospital, Devon said. He must have gone out on the ice and it gave. Just by accident one of the interns looking out from the second floor saw something where the hospital lights hit the water and he went out with two others to look. The boy was dead long before they carried him in. He's at the hospital now. I was with Martha. The police are going for Carmela, but I asked them to wait. Let Tom Verity tell her, I said, because— Because, Devon said.

And he took Tom to Carmela.

So it was Tom who told the end.

But who can know the moment that passed between Tom and

you, Carmela? Because Tom never said, would not. But whether you spoke or touched or merely sat together in that kitchen before anyone came to take you to identify your son, it must have been enough for you to answer that knock and stand face to face with Tom and see the look in his eyes to know all.

In town, only talk that day and the next and after the burial gave, gives, relief to this sorrow.

But it remains, the puzzle, deeply perplexing, of Brand's last run, so brief as to be unbelievable: from Tom's to the hospital, in that despair *I want her* and out onto the ice, an act which you must ponder and ponder, Carmela, as Tom ponders, and each of us ponders it: What reason? Is there ever one reason only?

In these days it may seem strange to see Tom halt in the middle of Center Street and stand and stare at your house on Third, standing as still as a monument, as if listening, waiting for some denial or revelation. At the instant of loss nothing, not even God, comforts. But Tom believes, and like you Tom is worn but must live with it—and speak to bear it—whisper the bits, fragments of his thoughts and intuitions, which feed the imagination, mine:

Again and again Tom must call *Wait, Brand!* and see the boy dash past the three houses to the hospital, wanting to see his teacher, but fearful—because he did not enter the hospital, maybe too ashamed to enter, feeling his guilt, *my friend Randy*, deceived and crying with disappointment and hurt and shame and insult and fury at his trust violated and, yes, his love violated, not even thinking or articulating *The key, I said where she hid it*, and *he* stole it, or Willis did; and Brand surely not even able to imagine the horror he knew only from the sound of Cash whispering *violated.*

So there was no recourse for him, that boy. He was so absolutely alone, as if *he* were that evil because he must have felt it was all his fault.

Tom said When he went out on the ice he must have wanted to die. I'm convinced that for one instant the boy became . . . must have been . . . was . . . .

Was? I said.

That Randy.

Randy Tidwell!

Yes, the Randy who will never exist, the part that's dead in him—because that boy did what no Randy Tidwell would ever do. Tom held the rolled cigarette, stared long at it, then at the little mechanical roller. His eyes quivered.

Yes, I said.

That poor boy, he murmured.

But what made him—? I said.

What? Tom said.

Nothing, I said.

How could that boy have known he was taking on Randy Tidwell's guilt and Willis Aken's and Devon and Martha's and town's and Tom's and mine and even yours, Carmela?

THE PRIVATE LIVES OF CHILDREN

For Marcy Lawton

Where are the children? They are scattered now, the five—to New York (Rick), Tennessee (Webb), Alabama (Rhea), Illinois (Brock), California (Fern), far from their birthplace in Rhode Island. In what house on what street now—Pine or Fourth or Calhoun or Milford or Wood? This town was theirs, their father's and fathers'. Where is the green cottage with the neat white trim? Where the shingled shed with its tools and rabbits, the loft and light and pigeons? Where the brook that flows by the house and under the little bridge over the road and into the meadow? Where the view of the harbor? Now condiminia stand, and no cows. No meadow but houses. The woods are pressed back and the harbor view shielded. Who of the five could then have imagined that he might stare from wrinkled skin and dry age at the same town. Gone? No. Old eyes lie. Their town will not die till they do. Town is an intimate island inside them, closer than blood, deeper than any well. They can never leave it.

This day is a big freeze. Even the harbor is frozen. You can cross on the ice. Good for eel fishing, Rick says. Rick, Ma says, you're the oldest. Watch the others, and stay where I can see you from the house. Pa'll watch us. We'll fish for eels in the brook, Rick says. You can come, Fern. But it's dark, Fern says. This is night fishing, Rick says, you carry the basket. Rhea says, I won't go, I won't kill them. Well, stick-in-the-mud, stay home, then, Rick says. I can cut holes in the ice, Brock says. Nothing doing, Pa says, I'll cut a hole for you, and you can do the rest. They cross the street and the swampy meadow, frozen solid, where Rick chooses a narrow, deeper part of the brook. Pa has a time cutting a circle in the ice. I'll be keeping an eye out, Pa says, but you be careful. Rick is fast. The trick is have the spear ready and when you shine the flashlight, before the eel can move, quick you spear it, Rick says. Uncle Jarvis taught me. You watch. Fern and Brock and Webb crouch around the hole. Do what I say. Rick is nine, and bossy. Flash the light—*now.* Zoom! Rick thrusts. It spears. The eel wriggles. Snake! Fern cries. She hates anything that wriggles. Come *on*, Fern, it's just a fish. Fern says, It moves like a snake. They're good to eat, Brock says. Fern says, I won't eat snakes. *You* caught it, you eat it. She wanders off with a flashlight. Part moon gives light, makes shadows. Behind, the voices sink quiet as if they don't want the eels to hear. She looks—still there, they are huddled a dark patch on the ice. The ice sort of glows. She follows the pond over the meadow. She shoots a few flashes. Fern, don't! Rick says, you'll scare the eels back up the stream. She says, Maybe I'll scare them right to you. She moseys over the ice slow, and halts because colors are clear through the ice, so clean, and then suddenly . . . Somebody? Face. A *face.* Like frozen, she stands still as it, staring, caught, but she's not afraid because it's under, or maybe she's fixed by fear but too curious to break free. Who? A man's face, closed eyes, and his hair dark and kind of wrapped over his forehead and his left ear, and like Pa only older. What're you doing here? she asks, not sure she didn't say it loud. She cuts the flashlight off. The face goes. Ice shines moon. She can't see through. She flashes light—yes, a face—quick shuts if off. The face stays in her eyes, still, clear, like a picture—and Rick calls, What you doing? Then Pa calls from far, Fern? Fern, Rick says, we got two, come see. She turns: They are the same, three around a hole, dark, and the bucket dark, and Pa dark by the stone wall. Rick is over the hole, and she sees, sudden, all their faces when Brock flashes the light. Now she's scared: They'll ask what she's doing, they always do because Ma's always saying, She's the youngest, keep an eye on Fern. But nobody asks anything. She's feeling heavy. She thinks she feels dizzy, but not, but sits anyway. Don't sit on the ice! Brock says, You'll get your ass wet. Don't! she cries. Mama says, There are words you don't say. I don't care what you hear, don't repeat them. The boys talk *eel* and *slippery*, and the long—*snout*, Rick says. *Jaws*, Brock says. *Mouth*, Webb says and Look how they coil. Fern looks: dark in the bucket. Poor things can't move, Webb says. Fern's seeing *him*, these eels *him*, he can't move. But she won't *say* to them. She won't tell. Secret. Keep a secret, Mama says. Is this a secret? She doesn't know secret, she never had a secret, but suddenly knows *secret*, mine, you don't tell. This must be, I won't tell it, my secret. Something you never let go, Ma says. She can't. She sees him. He's in her eyes, but not. It won't go. Maybe she can't let it. Secret. What Ma means. She trembles with it. You cold, Fern? Well, can't you talk? Get up, Rick says. And Webb: We'd better get home. If she catches cold, Ma won't let us come anymore. Why'd you sit on the ice anyway, Fern, huh? She stays clammed up. Let's go, Rick says. They cross the meadow, all crunches under their feet, the bucket handle creaking. She hangs last. She looks back. Secret. Where would it go? Where could it? How? Fern, Rick says, hurry up. Mama says, What luck! What talent my children have. Eels for supper? Brock says, That's why we caught them. I love fish. Me too, Rick says. When cooked, the house all fishy, Ma says, Fern, you're not touching your eels. Fern? I'm full up with potatoes. She won't touch the eel. They come from under the ice. From the face. They eat anything. Maybe they ate on the man. She won't eat. She won't eat on the man. She won't. Let *them*. At least, drink your milk, Fern. She drinks. Till bedtime the man lies still in her eyes. He's in her head. Her head is under the ice. In bed she sees him out the window in the pale sky, in the moony night. Up. High. She is with him, still, in the ice. Under. Nobody knows. Just me. Mine.

To the children time is green, is yellow, is a warm wind. Dandelions spread tiny yellow teeth. In the swamp in the meadow purple iris prod the air and unfurl and open deep throats with gold tongues. Tadpoles sprout quick legs. On the morning side of the house wind flags the yellow fire of forsythia. Daffodils are silent yellow trumpets. Trees put out yellow green in fine fingers that open and spread. Time is alive, it moves: New grasshoppers break from the dirt. Shadows glide over the ground and up trees. Sun slips down. Wind waves fields and water. Time moves in the waves of the harbor over their bodies, falls in snow turning slush and puddles, sounds in rain on the roof and thunder and the crunch of dead leaves, lashes in lightning, soars on the wings of butterflies, fireflies, dragonflies. It moves in skin, in the passage of faces, in the shifting of clouds, in their heights—Rick, Rhea, Brock, Webb, and Fern's—marked in inches on the wall.

At recess Rick sticks close to Alton. So what if he's Alton the Jew, the Jew Alton? He knows things, he's smart, the teachers know. One day Rick shows class his arrowheads. Alton says, I collect them too. You want to see mine? So home to Steinbergs'. The mother is dark and pretty. She stays all the time with them. Then the father. He puts his hand on Alton's head and musses his hair and kisses him and says, Tell me what's happening at school. Miss Landtree, you like her, what'd she do today? Took us on a safari to Africa. Don't tell me! And you're back the same day! That's something, hey, Sylvia? Mr Steinberg laughs, and Sylvia. You come anytime, Rick. And he feels Mr Steinberg's enormous hand cover his whole head, so warm, and his voice right in his hand goes all through him. He feels like peeing. And home, his mother says, They asked you in? surprised, and that night his father They usually don't. But, she says, that's when they're older, and don't mix boys and girls, you know, orthodox. And that night Rick dreams he falls into the brook beside the house but a hand grips him and pulls him up, but a drip down his leg wakes him and he quick gets up to pee. So at school is Alton, after school the two in the woods—except Friday: He can't go in and Alton can't come home with him. Synagogue. But God is Sunday, Rick says. Friday, Alton says, but calls Him another word. Rick has Brock and Webb and Rhea and Fern, but wants Alton and to go in and the hand. Pa asks things too and takes them on excursions but no hand or kisses, and Ma not often: because there are too many of us? Sometimes Mrs S sits on Mr S's lap and laughs. She kisses her boy and hugs. Rick hates Fridays because no Steinbergs. Mr Steinberg takes Alton, and not him. And God that other name takes Mr Steinberg with Mrs and Alton. He asks Alton one day What's that thing? Skullcap, my father's. You wear it in the synagogue, with Him. And once he dares to say to Mr S, Tell me the skullcap. Mr S laughs, but says, Come, and he is sitting on Mr S's enormous leg and he tells a long story about such respect and obedience and bowed heads and the East and humility and words he for the first time hears but is hearing the sound too, rich, of the voice, magic, and feels the heat and beating from Mr S, and his breath spilling on his skin warm and damp with a strong smell mixed with a clean smell of shirt and suit so he could close his eyes like he's Alton now and Mr S his father, two Jews whatever that means, and goes home after and in bed hears those words and says those words respect obedience humility over and over but to himself so Brock beside him and Webb in the other bed won't hear, the words are his. The days he and Alton go to the woods or Alton comes home with him or Fridays when he can't see Mr S but thinks Mr S and Alton at home with Mr S or just thinks Mr S, he sees *skullcap*, that black round cloth. Skullcap is Mr S, skullcap takes Mr S and Alton and Mrs S to the synagogue he has never been in, maybe can't go in, God that name keeping him out because no skullcap. He dreams it. Mine. On my head, so me Mr S and Alton and Rick in one skullcap. And Thursday—so they can't go to synagogue Friday, so he can be with them—Thursday when he is with Alton, he looks and looks until he sees it and all the time he waits for Alton not to look, to go to the bathroom, something, and takes the skullcap and jams it in his mackinaw, all of him shivering like sudden cold. This night he dares to take it out when Brock's sleeping and holds it, won't let it go, smells it, clutches it, stuffs it down in his pyjams, and morning puts it back in his mackinaw, thinking Got to find a place to hide it, thinking It's Friday, they can't go to that Word because I've got his skullcap, but after school it's the same, no Come in, but Tonight's synagogue, and he can't say, You can't go! so he leaves for home near crying, disappointed because no Mr S, no hand, but this, mine, this skullcap, and does not go right home but goes through the meadow across from the house and into the woods. He takes it out, he smells it, he holds it hard against his skin, he closes his eyes—that hand, the voice, the breath, nothing like his Sunday Him that Papa and Mama take him to because Mr S's hand voice breath make him quiver, make him Mr S and Alton and want never to move, only to feel and smell and hear Mr S and be Mr S and Alton and him. He knows his woods he plays in, the trees and bushes. He finds an old tree with a deep hole in the trunk. He hides the skullcap in it. He will never tell Mama or Papa or Brock or Webb or Fern or Rhea. He'll come every day. He'll change hiding places. When he leaves, he feels the skullcap like it's on his head. A hand. Synagogue. He is quivering.

Sound brings the five together, and their children, and theirs. They are never more than an instant away from voices, phoning, passing their lives into sound, and what more than their voices to invoke secret words never spoken, never to be spoken. Without being here, they come in, faces on a screen: Brock's grandson the astronaut spends twenty-one days in space doing experiments, his voice in all the world's rooms. Rick the biologist goes on an expedition with Cousteau to study deep sea plants. In the Communicable Disease Center in Atlanta Fern's oldest daughter works at disease control. *Out* imagination urges, *into*. Nobody can stop *out*. Earth has no down or up, but *out*. Space calls, once to other cities, towns, countries, and now the moon, planets, stars, universe. Their world shrinks. Sound and light draw each everywhere, together and alone. Nowhere is everywhere. Town inside them floats in space, penetrating farther and farther into space, with only sound and light to connect them in a web more fragile than a spider's. Yet when Rhea says, Remember when Fern fell from the shed loft, Fern falls, Fern is. If Brock reminds Webb how the brook flooded and drowned his rabbits, the flood comes, the rabbits drown.

> Mama tells Rick if he doesn't tend to his guinea pigs and get rid of some, he'll have to get rid of all of them, they multiply too fast and the pen isn't big enough for many more. Besides, there are Brock's rabbits and Brock's white mice, and the shed smells to high heaven. The apricots are ripe to falling and Webb and Fern help her collect them. Fern says Can we go now? She wants Brock. Brock is in the meadow across the street, chasing butterflies with a net. Brock is always collecting something. Come on, Webb. Ma calls out You stay away from the brook! Webb has come home soaked too many times. He's the smallest. The big kids sneak up behind and shove him in and scoot before he can even see who, but he knows who, the Connelly brothers older and big and tough and picking on him and calling him sissy. He gets covered with bloodsuckers he hates. Fern calls Brock, Brock! He's deep in the field of iris, an ocean of

purple heads with yellow mouths, and Fern runs deep in, the ground all damp and sucks and her feet quick wet. Come on, Webb! But Webb shakes no. He sits on the stone wall and watches Brock go after the big bright butterflies. Brock's fast, scoops and goes at it till he catches. He has a big mayonnaise jar he puts them in. Three this afternoon. He gets tired and hands Fern the net and he carries the jar home. Look, Webb. The wings are bright in the sun, so pretty, but hardly move, flutter weak. The three go out to the long bench in the shed. Mama says Keep all the creatures outside. Five of you are enough in the house. She laughs. Brock is careful. The colors are like dust; if you touch the wings colors come off on your fingers, so I keep them in the jar until—But they can't breathe! Webb says. That's right. You want them dead or so weak you can stick the pin through them.without wrecking the wings. Brock already has a half dozen pinned to a board with Ma's common pins. Brock says I'll show you. He uncovers the jar and careful dumps one out and his hand clamps its belly. The wings make a flap against the bench, and stop. Brock pierces it. Webb cringes. The pins go right through him. The butterfly gives a quick hard flap. Not dead yet, Brock says. Webb stares. It hurts. He wants to hit Brock, hit and hit. But stares. He watches the tiny string legs shiver. Here, you do it, Brock says, unscrewing the jar top again. Webb says, I'm going to the brook and without looking again crosses where the brook borders the yard. Ma calls out, Don't you go near the brook and keep out of the culvert. She is in the kitchen window over the sink. He keeps going—and climbs down the wall to the brook. He loves to walk the stones, cross the brook on them or follow them where it goes through the metal tunnel under the road and through the meadow. Green is always growing on the stones, fine threads and slippery. Hard to keep your balance. He goes a long time, but slips, up to his knees in the fast water, and climbs out the other side of the road, his shoes making a suck suck sound, and for a long time sits in the forget-me-nots all blue and watches bees and sometimes a grasshopper or little yellow butterflies but all the time mad at Brock killing butterflies, they can't fly now, and when he goes back to the yard, he waits and waits till Brock's not in the shed, nobody's in the shed, nobody, and knocks the board off and steps on the butterflies and then goes around the far side of the house to the front porch and sits to see if the old man the junk dealer will come by in his wagon with the horse and ask, Your mother got any junk today? Ask her. He does come by. The horse stops right in the street and three big turd balls drop from its behind. He runs and asks Ma. There's that broken wheelbarrow, Sam. And Sam puts it on his wagon and says, Much obliged, Mrs Farrow. You're more than welcome, Sam. Ma doesn't even see his wet feet. She says, It's almost suppertime. Everybody goes in but him and Fern—she's sitting on the front lawn trying to comb her long black hair with her fingers. So now Webb goes in. He can't stop being mad. Look at those shoes! Webb Farrow, you take those shoes off right now. You're tracking mud all over the kitchen. After supper they decide to play croquet. Rick and Brock go into the shed for the set. Suddenly Brock's making a real rumpus, shouting, My butterflies! Look at my butterflies! And Pa says, Well, I'm not surprised. Rats. There are turds all over the place. Don't be silly, dear, Ma says, field mice, they're everywhere. We don't have rats. I never saw one, Rhea says. Me either, Fern says. Webb says, We going to play croquet or not?

Awake, asleep, dreaming, something is moving in us, Brock says. The future is alive in us; sperm and egg, it waits, Rick says. It wills to break out of us into something else. We are passing through, Rhea says. Webb the bachelor says, I am a dead end, where motion exits into motion. We are snow and rain and fog,

Fern says. We carry the light of stars, Brock says. We are dust that moves and will one day lie still, Rick says. The family lives in us, Webb says, we are history. Living or dead, Rick says, we will float farther and farther out, still but moving, and forever. What we discover out there will be what we carry in us, Rhea says.

Rhea is "Gramp's girl" because the first girl grandchild. Gramp never says so but Brock has heard Mama say it to Papa. Times when Gramp says, Who'll I take to the farm, all five want to go but they know *two*, only two each time. So now's Rhea's turn, and Brock's. Gramp raises peacocks. Useless things, Mama calls them, and ugly, but beautiful when they spread their tails, and mean, and they make the sorest screech ever heard. But Brock and Rhea love all the eyes like sudden spies on them, but more love escaping to the silo and climbing forbidden in when the fodder's being cut and pouring down like hard rain on them, it could bury them, they scream with joy, they could smother, but climb and climb as it pours in and piles higher and higher under them, till finally they crawl back up the ladder and out the opening—saved!—just like in the Saturday serial at the Pastime. Mostly they follow Gramp—through the barn and cow smell past the giant milk cans and into the building where they make ice cream to sell. And Mrs Smith always invites them in and tells the kitchen girl to set the table: Time for a hot lunch for the children and Mr Verity, but calls Gramp Tom when they're talking. After, Brock sticks close to Gramp as he can. In the chicken coop Gramp says, One of you can scrape the muck aside, handing a hoe. Me, Brock says, though Rhea doesn't seem to care because she collects eggs with Gramp. Rhea loves eggs. She runs her fingers soft over the eggs like they're already chicks and places each carefully in the basket. Brock knows they don't help much but Gramp likes them happy. You can play in the meadows but don't abuse the cows and be careful you don't step in the turds, your mother'll have a fit, and if you go to the woods, don't go so far in you can't hear me call. But don't go down the cliff to the beach, I can't see you down there. We'll go down when all the family comes with the church for sunrise service Easter. The farm is a long stretch of rocky land right to the edge of the bay and almost down to the end of town, the point in the bay, and the bridge that crosses to an island. They can never go near water without Mama or Papa or Gramp or some grown-up. Let's go to the woods. You go, she says, I'll stay with Gramp. She picks weed flowers all colors. So he goes furious to the woods. He'd like to get lost or hide and make them look and look, or meet a wild animal, too bad no wolves, anything to make Gramp come. He hunts mushrooms, two pockets full, then thinks Maybe they're poison, Ma can tell when she puts a quarter in when they're cooking and it changes color. He's so mad he could poison Rhea right now. He knows Ma won't have them so he dumps them. By the house Gramp is resting. Rhea's been collecting weed flowers and has an old jam jar and wants water for them. Gramp doesn't use the faucet but goes to the old well Mrs Smith won't fill in and lets her lower the bucket and, part full, wind it back up—Rhea always loves that—and she fills the jar and arranges the flowers she wants to take home to Ma. Smell, Gramp. Gramp says, They don't smell. She laughs. They make your throat yellow. Gramp says, That's sun on the buttercups. Anything, Brock thinks, to get her away from Gramp. Gramp's peacocks, thirty Gramp says, are all over the yard—perched and sitting and standing and walking. He thinks, I'll fix them. Brock wants to do, *do*—get Gramp away, fix *her*. He takes out his slingshot, and from the far side of the yard, behind them, lets a peacock have a pebble smack in its rump: it screams and charges off. He does one more, and fast shoves the slingshot into his pant waist. By now Gramp is standing, confused, and Rhea scared by the rush of peacocks scooting scared all over the yard, racing toward Gramp and Rhea. Gramp walks in the middle. He knows his birds. Rhea follows close behind him, scared when they all flutter around Gramp and run almost smack into them. She flaps her arms and some pick at her arms and legs and neck and face and she screams and screams and closes her eyes and flags her arms screaming Gramp! Gramp! and that makes the birds pick worse and then she covers her face with her hands and they come away blood. She screams My eye! My eye! And Gramp shoos the birds, Git! Git!, gripping her and examines and says, Not your eyes, thanks be. It's Rhea's neck. A bird has torn a good piece from her neck and it bleeds and bleeds. Brock is scared. By now Mrs Smith and the girl Liz come running out and Gramp carries her though she can sure walk by herself and in no time they are all inside and Mrs Smith washes the tear and puts something on it—strong, Rhea cries—and then the bandage and adhesive tape. I don't know what got into those birds, Gramp says. Peacocks are strange, Mrs Smith says. Who knows better than you, Tom? Outside, Gramp sets Rhea on his lap and smokes a cigarette. When time comes to go home, he carries her piggyback to the car. Ma is flustered. I'm taking you straight to Doctor Bernardo. And Brock's all fury and worried too, because *that cut*. Like she'd die from it, but didn't, won't! Days and days after, no more bandages but a long wide dark streak on her neck, the left side. It'll shrink a little, Ma says, but she'll always have a scar. A scar? Brock asks. Something for always, Ma says. A scar, Brock says.

Rhea has four sons, scattered, and seven grandchildren. In a nursing home on Long Island Rick, except in rare lucid moments, does not recognize his wife and two daughters or the granddaughter who visits faithfully or the other two sometime visiting grandchildren. At the Nashville station, after all the passengers leave the train, a conductor finds Webb Farrow sitting still and upright in a coach, victim of a stroke. Fern flies Webb from the hospital home with her to La Jolla. Webb sits, a still face haunting the bougainvillaea. Brock's only grandson dies in the Korean war. Two of Rhea's are MIAs in Vietnam. At a University of Chicago commencement, Brock receives in his brother Webb's name the honorary degree for his achievement in entomology. What, Brock wonders, is this "like your father," "like your grandmother," "like your great-grandfather," like those unnameables who carried millennia of genes? What is this pattern? Why is it? This tree found in every leaf, nerve system, insect, man?. Rigid this order? In what surrounding chaos? All—insects, trees, men—feed on feeding. Are we the virus of all viruses? Who are Rick Rhea Brock Webb Fern RickRheaBrockWebbFern rickrheabrockwebbfern? What is this relentless *and dna* and/dna/and/dna *anddnaanddnaand . . .*?

Katherine Hamilton, Kat, Kathy, Katie they call her, but the kids K.D., that's how they say Ka-dy. K.D. lives three houses away and always stops to talk if anybody's on the porch. Weekdays she passes at 5:15 on the way home from work at the School Board. Rhea likes her clean smell of soap and sweet hair and the voice so creamy soft it whispers inside her. K.D. one day when Rhea is biting her pencil over division, K.D. says, Let me show you, and K.D. does five examples slow and clear, in steps, and the soap and sweet and warm breath and close skin make it so comfy easy. So at five weekdays Rhea waits on the steps just to see her and hear Hi, Rhea and those high heels Ma calls spikes she wears to church Sundays. K.D. goes to service too, but Rhea and Fern and Rick and Brock and Webb go to Sunday school and to rec till church is out and then she sometimes sees K.D. and her father the judge she lives with, the mother dead. Rhea can't wait to grow into K.D.'s class, but years yet. She prays, Years, please go fast. And one noon Ma says Judge Hamilton must miss his wife even more on holidays. I've made him a pumpkin pie, but can't go, your father's stopping by the Balsams', you take this to Hamiltons', Rhea. Ma sets it in a round basket and covers it with a white cloth napkin. Careful! It's hot. Don't knock against anything. Don't go in. And come straight back. Your father will be here any minute and we'll eat. But before she knows it, she's inside—she can't resist when K.D. laughs all white teeth and so happy to take the pie and press her into the big house, dark with lamps lit in day. My father's resting. You sit there. I've a little thing for you children. Rhea is all racing eyes: on pictures painted and rugs and big dark furniture with streaks of light and glass bright and too many objects ever even to see half before a cat, My Siamese, Ini, slips silky behind her legs. Then K.D. says, Take this for all of you. The chocolate smell right through the box makes her mouth water. Ooooh! Rhea is pins and needles, says, Thank you, says, I can do division good now, and lots more. She stands up. Oh, you can't run on me, K.D. says. Wouldn't you like to see where I live? Ma says—But K.D. has her arm: It won't take long, so the next time you'll feel at home. And Rhea is going through rooms so high she's a dwarf, and wide as Moses' Red Sea Miss Cullen told about, and long stairs in half a circle and dark the corridors and more and more space, fireplaces with logs, and at every turn she sees herself going right to herself in enormous mirrors catching windows behind her, only one door they pass closed, the judge's, and upstairs they go outside through windows to the floor—My balcony where I read, K.D. says—and Rhea can look all up and down the street and to the woods on one side and over the meadow and brook and the cove beyond and the harbor and boatyards like all the world is in your eye. And there is her own house, so small from here and hiding in the trees. And they go inside and up higher still: This is where I used to play by myself when I was little. I made up people. You do that? No, Rhea says, I've got too many home. K.D. laughs. Lucky you. I made mine. See all those dolls I made. Rhea's surprised: so many, and toys, little stages, puppets—and nobody there now, just dolls for nobody. And Rhea wants to sit and never leave, but remembering Pa'll be home in a minute says, Ma'll be mad if I'm late. They go a different way down through a kitchen for giants, this place lots of windows and all the pots and pans hanging high from beams and shiny. At the door she's holding the chocolates and praying K.D. will find a way to keep her, not let her leave. But: Ma's waiting. K.D. says, Thank your mother. We love her baking. She never forgets us. And, Rhea, you come whenever you want to. K.D. kisses her on top of the head. And lets her out. She is burning. She is to burst. She runs. Breathless, she says, I went in, I saw the house, big as the ocean. Ma laughs. It *is* grand. And says softly, But I told you never to go in, Rhea. I couldn't say no. Well, next time, dear you say no. We mustn't bother the judge. So now more, on time, Rhea won't miss 5:15 day and day and day and at church, a glimpse. And then on a day, Tuesday—nobody. Wednesday—and nobody. Where is she? She wants to go up the street, up the drive, knock on the door to the big house: Why don't you come? But can't say Ma says *forbidden.* No word, nothing Rhea'll say. Can't. But about to bust. Till Thursday. Pa, with his I'm-talking-to-your-mother voice, low, hard to hear, and always words hard to make sense. She. It takes time to know they are talking *She.* She, Pa says, is not there anymore. Listening, Rhea thinks, Not at the house? And Ma says, Not at work? Dismissed, Pa says. Rick says, Rhea, you going to buy Park Place or not? Don't take all night. And Pa: They're not going to press charges because of the judge. They certainly won't make a scandal of it, nobody wants that—it's bad enough as it is—but it borders too much on indiscretion and, though I would be unable to condemn her nature, it is just to condemn her conduct. Her! Her! Her! Rhea knows from their lows, their voices, the *hides* in their sound, something bad has happened because *disappeared*, she *has*. She doesn't pass Park Place. She wants to get up, run to that house, and bang and ask K.D., what what what? Why don't you come? She can't ask—she knows that. She can hardly keep from crying. She says, Brock, you want to play Monopoly? Take my place. She quits. And more days go. The porch at 5:15, habit. She knows *she*—who's not K.D. anymore but *she*—won't come but prays, Send her, God. But God doesn't, nobody does. She sits. *They*, now, hardly mention K.D. But one night Pa says, They've sent the girl off to a private school and it seems the end of the matter. Matter? Once Ma said, Pus is matter, when she squeezed Webb's swollen finger and pus shot out. But this matter is trouble. Their voices tell it. And another sitting, 5:15 till supper. And for sure now Ma knows. Ma touches her hand, her shoulders, says, Come, hon, help me roll the crust. And the next afternoon We're having a cold buffet supper so let's all go down to see what's going on at the Cove—and they don't get home till near six when Pa comes. Ma says, You want to cut the pie, Rhea? Ma keeps her close a lot. She loves Ma. But she *wants*. And wants to be alone. And first time she can, when the others are across the street in the meadow catching tadpoles for Brock's class, and Ma busy with the vac, Rhea quick goes out with scissors and cuts Ma's new tea roses, a bunch, then puts the scissors back, and races up to the other block that's all the judge's and crosses the drive to the house and bangs the knocker and waits a long time, waits, but nobody. But waits. She wants to cry, Come, K.D.! And thinks she hears sound, maybe voices. But nobody comes. And she does cry. She stands with the roses in her arm and is crying. *Now* what will I do with them? Clutching the roses—they prick—and crying. And hears a faint sound: a tapping. And looks up. She! Her face in the narrow window beside the door. *She's* crying! Rhea can tell. She. Her own head

> and chest and legs are beating. She could scream, happy and hurt because *she's* there, but her eyes red and crying too. Why? Both of them crying. And *she* shakes No. No? And Rhea knows *she* can't either—forbidden?—so holds up the roses, and *she* nods, and Rhea leaves the roses on the stoop by the door and waves and turns and runs like never before, afraid she might hear No, hear her voice, hear the word *No.* And it is not till the next day that Ma says she is *mortified* to think anybody would be so bold as to come right into the yard and steal the first roses of the season: and Rhea nothing, no word, never to tell *her*, her face, her eyes, those tears, that No, and roses.

Time is white, Fern thinks. Ice. And a face frozen still. Her own stillness moves. Some instants, she lies under ice, still, with *him.* Brock sees the moment on Rhea's neck. When Rhea touches the scar, Brock and she are young, with the peacocks and Gramp. Webb sees butterflies pinned to Brock's board. Did dead butterflies, he wonders, lead me to this life of detecting and saving species? Time, Brock says, is fallen hairs in the sink. Where, Rick wonders, is the skullcap? Was it food for some creatures? He sees that tree, the wood, the house. How many times, in stillness, Rhea thinks, I walked up the street to the judge's door. What is this lifetime of waiting? What is it that has not happened? Something . . . inside, too far to touch? Why too far, if inside? If I could name it! If I could say, but *what* say? The face in the window. Tears. Roses.

I'LL NEVER LEAVE YOU

Old Julius points. Dolphins!

Far out in the Sound, their dark backs break the surface like moving hoops.

Alan stirs in his rocker. His hand reaches out toward them. The promise, he says.

Promise? Julius's daughter-in-law, Elsa, looks mystified.

Dolphins rescued sailors from drowning by riding them ashore on their backs, or so the myth goes, Mom, Anne says.

I'd like to ride one, Alan says. His voice is a bare whisper. He stares out to sea, smiling.

Oh, Anne, you know everything, Elsa says.

Anne laughs. Don't all professors? Gramp taught me. Didn't you, Gramp? she says to Julius. You made me see the Sound's a living body, and the Island, and everything's dependent, everything's one. Oh, I wish I knew half of what's in that head of yours. She kisses it.

Julius's hands reach for her face.

The old man is tall, thin, all fiber, a sturdy weed, his tongue withered but not his mind. Since his stroke he can utter only syllables, a word, two, fragments. Still, Anne always talks the latest on salt marshes or horned owls or barnacles and takes him in the car and parks at his favorite places for exploratory walks or reads to him when she's home. And the family makes their usual talk with Julius as if nothing has ever happened. All the years Alan has loved Julius, Steve's father, like his own.

Anne is home from the university because Alan wants her here this weekend. He did not have to say. Her father knew. Steve always knows. Steve knows all his desires. Only Steve knows. He always has, a lifetime.

But weeks ago it was Elsa who, when she saw Alan pallid and weak in his own bed in Mattituck, told him, You're coming home with us right now. No, no, don't put up a fuss. You're not staying here by yourself. You can't. If your best friends can't take care of you, Alan Peabody, who can?

If no family, he thought, who but a housekeeper and aides?

Because he could no longer hide *dying*.

So, as for Sunday dinners all the years with them, here he is, where he wants to be, and forever. Time, if relentless, seems to have turned back.

Morning sun makes the Connecticut shoreline a stark sculptured trail between water and sky. Close, the Sound heaves and falls in great, slow, silver breaths. Isolated gulls stand motionless, too bright against the sand.

Elsa puts her hat on, the wide-rimmed straw with its aqua band and two tiny pheasant feathers. Sunday she will not do without God and St. Mary's and loves the nuns. Private and uncondemning, she has kept Catholic, the only one in the house, and in silence always observes and will not neglect.

Ready? Steve is suddenly standing there, always a startle with his strong swagger as if he'd just swung off his tractor, middling, but still so rugged hard you could think he is twenty and his face as young if you keep some distance; but his eyes anxious now on him, Alan, as never over the years; he knows Steve hates this sickness that so breaks a friend and the world of tomorrow which you dare not turn your face toward—for Steve's still glance and his patience all his life have been almost a reserve in him, easy to live with but hard to know: everybody likes him and admires the worker in him and respects him for his friendly distance if not for the stranger he guards within.

We won't be long, Elsa says. The words are for him, Alan, and her glance, assuring.

Anne is carrying Julius step by step through her slow experience over a Connecticut berm to mark ospreys with numbered lock-on bands. They have diminished to a few dozen there now. Julius's eyes grow wide as an owl's. He turns to Alan. Duss—nnnnns, he says. Julius won't leave him out; Julius, who is also so near *the other side*, would keep Alan here too. Mu—ssscc? Julius says, indicating the stereo, for who for an instant forgets the history of Alan's passion? Not right now, Alan whispers. Nothing of the rich tenor is left in his voice. But *their* voices . . . How can they know their voices are music? Smiling, he stares out to sea, listening, and soon sinks, submerged in other sounds. This natural music. After all the years, now so acute is his ear that when alone, far from these sounds, his imagination can conjure them up, let himself sink comfortably into them. Lying still, standing motionless, he sinks under wind, under waves. They come, the finest sounds: the chafe of a fiddler crab's big male claw while mating, chafing grains of sand, a horseshoe crab moving over stones underwater, the fall of a beach rose petal, a dragonfly flit, the suck of a lilypad, scud moving, reeds quivered by wind. Unheard melodies . . . .

Who knows what music you may hear?

It is as if now he has gone back to *once*, that almost mythical time before change of voice, before voice lessons and scholarships and auditions, before the discovery of his "extraordinary tenor," which was the promise of the Met, La Scala, the Colón before his rejection of that "God-given gift," his *no* to the world he'd spent years preparing himself for. That rejection had been a mystery to everyone. At the time, people would pass by the bank merely for a glimpse of him. After all, you did not reject the promise of such a future. Privately he had achieved the promise; what he had rejected was fame, publicity, invasion. But people's puzzlement soon died, or retreated to casual speculation.

Once. Yes, but *once* was the boy with that pal his dog, Edge. Named for the sand cliff we live on, he'd explain, between clouds that some days pressed dark faces down close or clear blue you could fall up into, and sand, and the water that you could see turn harsh or soft, unpredictable but not so unpredictable as people: so he turned, alone with Edge, to the crick or bay or harbor or Sound, a wanderer on foot or in his rowboat, or alone with crabs and fish and swimming scallops in the shallows, and by the crick and cemetery with black snakes and fish hawks and herons and the myriad birds and beavers and rats and, alone, listened—it was the once of primitive music that was gone and forever except when, alone now, he closed his eyes and listened to echoes within, exiled from now to the exile of then: because already then he was waiting; he did not know he was waiting or for what, but waiting. He was interested only in the moment, to follow each thing that moved—what moved it?—and he'd stare at what moved and listen to its motion and feel it move in himself, that primitive music.

He was more fish than not. He had his casual friends but no one friend. He kept to himself and the Sound and marshes and woods and always books—and then was his voice, that discovery and passion that fed the hours of his life and consumed them and fixed him, an exile to opera: You know all life is opening its great door for you.

If any, his first music teacher, Miss Germaine, was his confidante—all stirrings of doubt she dispelled in the name of the necessary sacrifice. Often her gray hair, her thin face pale in its exhausted beauty, her swan neck cord-thin then, but most her eyes that sought distances made him wonder what sacrifice had brought *her* to this town of two thousand. Her image has never left him.

She is standing here now.

He hears her: One day everything you've turned your back on, all you've yearned for and needed will come. . . . Her voice was an anguish of desire and despair, and her fingers hard on his, so he knew, but did not know yet what he knew. He would see such despair in her once more years later on the day back in town when he went to tell her—he had to, he owed that to her—that after the years and the work, the willing slavery, at the moment of signing his contract he balked and withdrew—everyone was sure he was having a nervous breakdown, but he was too determined and serene—but that time, in her tiny rented apartment behind the grocery converted to the Jehovah's Witnesses hall, she broke from her stillness, her face incredulous, her eyes went wet, she clutched her own face, she quivered and shrank, her drained hope left her pale, and if Why? Why? was first on her mind she did not ask, maybe dared not, maybe he was too much she at that moment, too much some of her past latent in him, which had always threatened her too. He had no need to tell her or anyone: *Because I'll never leave here.*

Yes, he is where he wants to be.

He has loved, loves, this house. Home. His grandfather had it built for his wife. It stands high toward the cliff and apart from town but visible from the long road, commanding the fields he'd inherited, acres and acres of corn and potato and cauliflower, more and more of it each year being transformed to vineyard. Alan's parents and grandparents, lawyers or educators all, like Steve's did not farm but leased it. But Steve broke tradition—he loved the land and outdoor work, mastered machines, studied agronomy; he came home from the university with a passion to make the land his: to see him work you'd think he was wrestling with a living thing. To him it is, it breathes human.

Is your throat dry, Alan?

Elsa!

He is startled: because in his musings there is no Elsa yet. Now in an instant twenty-five years vanish as quickly as a breaking wave, and where?

He realizes: Mass is over?

Oh, it's never long. Father Rego sends his blessing. And—you won't believe it—I even persuaded Steve to listen from the lobby.

Steve!

Who believes in blood and sap and the impulses of the irrational world.

Yes.

And who affirms it now by laying a hand on his shoulder.

Pole, Julius says.

Anne says I was telling Gramp the osprey still returns to his nest on top of that tilted old electric pole rotting by the Widow's Hole. Shall we go have a look, Gramp?

Julius nods with vigor.

Shall we take the dog? Anne calls Lord.

Beside Alan, the Lab raises its head. So like, Lord could be Edge.

Fat chance. He won't budge, Elsa says. He's Alan's right hand. Steve'll take him for a run later.

Alan runs his hand over the dog's head. Lord presses against it, his eyes closing, and releases a deep sigh of ecstasy.

After, Anne says to Julius, We'll circle around by Pete Neck for what we can spot in the sea grass. We'll be back in plenty of time for dinner.

They're a pair! Elsa says. Seems only yesterday that Julius used to head out carting Anne on his back. Now she's leading him. Why, look—Julius seems to be laughing.

That's pure love. Alan's own laugh comes husky.

Steve sits, rises, moves to the deck door and raises his arms and grips the jamb and, stretched, seems to hang there.

You're losing weight, Alan says.

Tell him, Alan, Elsa says.

There's no need for that, Steve.

Steve is silent.

Or for worry, Alan says. We've decided that. We could begin by having a drink—to encourage your appetite, and mine.

Steve drops his arms and turns to face him. A drink?

What's wrong with our having a drink before dinner? Alan says.

Before Steve can reply, Elsa says, That sounds like an order to me, Steve.

Wine. I'll have a little wine, Alan says, yes.

Two. There's Beaujolais, Elsa says. You mix what you want, Steve. And pour ours?

You're sure, Alan? Steve says.

Sure? Alan purses. What's sure? Move. And he hears his own throat clutch that laugh. Didn't Doctor Lux tell you, Give him anything he wants?

Elsa sets up a tray beside him. Close, her flesh is sweet, of some flower, yes, lilac.

And my house? he asks, though he feels that his house, his possessions, the view of the inlet have vanished, imagined, because isn't he beginning this life—imagined once—now, here? No, not I beginning. *We* are. Have we backtracked to begin? Are the imagined and the real the same life? Or do they come together at some point?

Your place is as clean as a whistle. I see to that myself.

You! You don't have to, Elsa.

That's why. She smiles a wifely smile. Hasn't she given him, years now, the comfort of a wife, his but not his? Her full figure, firm, verges on matronly now, this long-legged once slim daughter of a German immigrant, who worked in the potato fields and sold vegetables at her family's roadside stand after school, her blonde hair almost concealed under a bandana, at school always with a kind of sun-filled laughter, her white teeth sudden, her head tilted in curiosity—something soft and restful in her attracted. A worker dot one, her father would proudly say, got head dot one. No wonder Steve told the family, the first year he came home from agronomy, I've found the complete woman right here under my nose and I've never really seen her until now. What more?

That year Alan's mate was his voice; voice his life, blood, obsession. He seldom went home from New York—for a holiday, yes, or a family illness, and sometimes from a rare, inexplicable, emotional eruption.

Do you want something on the stereo, Alan? He knows: Elsa does not want him to talk, not strain. Mozart?

No. The waves are enough, their sound.

Well, nothing's so restful.

In no time Steve is back with wine. Alan can hardly hold the glass. The wine shimmers crimson in his hand. He sips. Quick fire burns through him. The sea blurs.

I could pitch a good drunk with this. A laugh catches in his throat.

You never would in your life! Steve says.

You wouldn't either, Elsa says. For Steve is all health, discipline, order. You can't have any real fun without control, he always says. And Elsa says, But letting yourself go at the right time is part of the control. You'd be as insane not to let yourself go as you would be to let yourself go all the time, wouldn't you?—Elsa arches coyly—though *I've* never gone that far. Right now, *if* we're going to have Sunday dinner this afternoon, I'd better go—with control—to the kitchen. She laughs.

In an instant there comes the sound of cabinet doors, metal on metal, crockery.

Actually Elsa is uncomfortable doing nothing, and Steve too, though since they brought him here, both have hovered close, Steve trying to disguise his worry, inventing tasks close to the house, avoiding the field, farming more tasks out to hired help. Alan tells himself he should feel guilty, but he wants them here, revels in their presence, in the sound of Elsa in other parts of the house, of Steve about the house and grounds, of their frequent "casual" runnings in and out of his room or the living room when he's gazing out to sea. He has become an island that they move about, that places them, like one of those boulders the waters swirl about on the beach below:

Down there, where his life began.

Remember Edge? Alan laughs, coughs.

Remember! You trickster, Steve says.

But it was Edge, not Steve, he had been trying to trick. He hardly knew Steve or Elsa then, though both had been a year behind him in high school. It was during one of those returns from the City when he was feeling so alien to everything that he went swimming in the Sound, there in the waters below the house. He had ducked under. He stayed under, swimming almost to bursting. Even underwater he could hear Edge's barking, muted. Suddenly a body came up beside him and clutched him and hauled him up, startled and lashing. Steve Mitchell! You okay? Steve said. Alan burst into frenzied laughter. Didn't the whole town know he'd been a champion swimmer? It was his only sport. And Steve a three-letter man. I was teasing Edge by staying under. Steve stared up at him a long instant, his face clouded, then laughed and released him. Edge bounded from him to Steve, and lapped Steve. You're getting your thanks, Steve. They sat on the sand. I've read about you several times, Alan. That's because my mother sees to it that the local reporters earn their pay, Alan said. Well, Steve said, it's nothing easy you're doing. Easier for me, Steve, than what you're doing! But farming's my life. and I can't sing! And Alan said, I read you and Elsa Landowski are headed the way of all flesh. In September, yes—my great moment, Steve said. This is great too. I don't have much drama in my life. Alan laughed. Steve, suddenly, rather self-consciously, stood. Edge looked from one to the other questioningly. You've made a friend, Steve. Steve petted him: See you, Edge. Steve! Alan called. Steve halted and turned. Thanks for the rescue. Steve laughed. Whose? He stood staring an instant and then went on.

Alan's mother kept him up on town, sent the weekly, but he wouldn't have remembered reading about the wedding if Edge hadn't died that week. And, fleetingly, it associated Edge with Steve. *Edge*. His mother had called: Your father buried him where you always said you wanted him, his favorite spot in that little corner of the garden by the tool shed. *Buried?* Edge had been *all those years, town, the Sound, me.* Buried. In me. As long as Edge had been there, he knew he had not imagined that time; suddenly it was hard to believe it had been real. Rifted. Edge had been his, his companion. Always those soft dark eyes fixed on him, loving, Edge ready at his least motion to move with him, tongue out, his mouth open as a warm smile. What tied him to the place then? Memory? But you couldn't touch memory. And he yearned to touch.

He buried his yearning in his obsession with his voice. When his uncle Ned called to tell him his parents had been killed in a car wreck at the notorious fork on the back road in Southold, he closed up the house but would not sell it—dared not: he felt his life so confined that without having *somewhere* he could go, he might come to believe that that life too had been imagined. Its presence kept part of him in town. Had a dormant part of him been waiting to be quickened? Summers, if rarely and briefly, he dared step back into that life, an alien in his own memory.

Until Elsa. Who ran into him grocery shopping in the IGA.

Alan! It's been years. Remember? Elsa Landowski—Mitchell now. Steve and I have read of your wonderful life. How exciting it must be! Come by, please. Have dinner with us one night? Better, I'll send Steve by. I know he'd like to see you. He's never forgotten the day of the dog!

Edge! He laughed. But it revived that moment, vivid.

Elsa and he took to each other at once. Steve, quiet, watched, listened: because Alan, startled at himself, was suddenly a talker, like Elsa: before she'd married she'd loved getting away from this tip of the Island and "going west" to "the City"; reveled in the ethnic mix; felt free in the crowd; yearned for the Met, plays, symphonies; prowled the Village; even dared Harlem! You bring it all back, Alan. Oh, yes, she'd loved it, but loved the farm more; her roots were deep; she was born for space, this flat land, endless sea; even the naked monotone of winter had its bold beauty.

Sunned dark, his eyes startingly white, his chestnut hair tinged rich reddish streaks, thinner, if rugged and hard, Steve, inactive, always looked uncomfortable relaxing: his body was made for work. Yet, if their conversation flagged, he wouldn't let it die: Your father set my broken leg. And my mother always said she wouldn't have any lawyer but your grandfather. All I remember is his beard.

So their Sunday dinners came to be.

At the end of August she said, This has been *my* summer. How I'll miss you, Alan. What a change you've made in our days. Hasn't he, Steve?

The days have to go on, don't they, Alan? he said.

Oh, Steve! she said. Killjoy!

Or realist.

Alan laughed: Well, the City's practically in your backyard. You *could* find it!

But he was not prepared: a night that fall the porter buzzed him—

Steve Mitchell was below.

Steve!

At once he thought *Elsa*.

Something's happened . . .?

Happened? Oh, no, no. I'm in to Brooklyn for a farm machinery fair . . . . The convention ends noon tomorrow and I had the night free, so I thought here's the chance, I'll run in to the City for an hour or two. . . . You *said* find you.

So the Island had come to him, it stood there in Steve Mitchell. Home. But why this exhilaration?

The joy released him. Not given to talk, he let talk out as if in a burst, unable to contain words so long hoarded: through drinks and a walk through the crowd and dinner at the little Italian restaurant where he sought his usual nook. Why was he talking? Was he afraid not to? Was he afraid of his own silence? And all the time Steve was silent, but his eyes so alive, restless over him, listening, or watching, this man who belonged in the fields, whose hands loved soil, whose body loved sun and wind and, yes, who loved silence too. And he, Alan: Was he drowning Steve in words? Was he giving the illusion of rushing time away, rushing the night only to free himself?

Steve, standing in the window, looking out over the lights, said, It's too much for me.

Alan came up behind. You'd get used to it.

I've tried, Steve said.

Alan was mystified. Tried?

I can't. Alan . . .

Then Alan felt Steve's hands move back and slide over his thighs and grip his legs behind and draw him close against his back, his head slumped back against Alan's neck, and he said in an almost stifled whisper I can't, I've been afraid to come but I had to. Alan . . .

And Alan held him, held, felt *This*, like holding his own body palpitating to madness. He could not contain this—

Steve . . .

That night he knew Steve, the soft Steve that lay against him, yielding, that roused and roused him to taking, who all night lay close against him, held, one body, till in the morning he dreaded the rift—still, he looked at Steve new, the room new, the world out there new.

Now, dressed, Steve took on his old self, the new self hidden except in his warm gaze, his smile, the hand on him. He said, Everything's changed. I'll never be the same again.

You want to be, Steve?

Never.

Do you think I do?

If you do, last night didn't mean anything.

Then . . .? Alan didn't know how, after this . . . revelation, *he* could go back to yesterday. I'll have to live with that, Steve said. I can, I want to, but if I don't see you again . . .

Don't see me!

Because you'll be gone all over the world.

I'll always have to come back here.

Well, *if* we don't see each other, if it doesn't ever happen again . . . .

It *will*. Steve!

But Steve closed the door and Alan heard his steps swift along the corridor to the elevator, going away from him. . . . , leaving him already with a memory, which would fade, which he might eventually believe he had simply imagined.

He couldn't let that happen!

So began the return to his house weekends whenever he could go, and holidays, vacations—living for an hour or two with Steve; for a touch; for the sight of him in the field or on the street; and with Elsa too because it was Elsa who lured: I've made something special just for you. Steve needs visitors, he works too hard, he's a different person with company. Besides, *I* want you here. Doesn't that mean anything?

Everything it meant: because when he took Steve, he embraced Elsa too now. If at first when it had happened he felt he was betraying her, violating her life—he was!—it was Steve who said Maybe destroying's part of creating. Part of love? Love? It's not love—I mean I love Elsa and I love you, but what I feel for Elsa and you, it's more than love, more powerful—call it love, I don't know what it is. It's a curse, but a fortunate curse. Sometimes alone in the field I want to cry out to the earth or the sky or the air, What's the secret? Tell me, because there's such a madness, there's a frenzy in the corn, the potatoes, in us, in some of us more than others—why?—and some can't live without living it, not to is to be half dead, and who wants to die? I don't. You and Elsa—you've brought me to life, I want life, I want Elsa, I want children, and I want you, I can't be myself without both of you. . . .

Because Steve, this rugged hard body, would succumb; Steve would lie in his arms, turn soft, let his body yield with a primitive feminine hunger to the strength in him, a latent masculine drive for years obsessively channeled to cultivate his tenor, but now . . . He had never known this.

And then Elsa: You're going to be a godfather, Alan!

Anne.

And *Roland* a year later.

They're as much yours as ours, she'd say. And they were, they *were.*

And would it end, this? He feared the end, if not the end the constant interruptions, the long vacancies when he would be in Rome or Paris or Vienna without Steve, without Elsa and the children, without town, the Sound, the house . . . and why? Standing in the window, looking out, listening to the hush-hush of the waves, thinking I know where I am, I know where I want to be, where I belong, I know who I am, he thought, Then *why?* because the moment he had anticipated for years, and now dreaded, was here: Next week he must sign the contract. His *life*, after so many years of discipline and sacrifice, was to begin. Begin? But in an instant's revelation life *had* begun. He was living it. And to end that? That would be death.

And he would not die.

He thought, It was not for nothing Steve tried to rescue me from the Sound that day with Edge.

Now, looking out over the waves, with Steve beside him, he sees that moment clearly: when he said The time's come, Steve. If I sign, I'll be gone most of the time—

If! What do you mean *if*? You've worked years for this. You deserve it. How many people in the world are born with such a voice? You can't deny the world—

But he heard too the despair in Steve's voice, in his eyes he saw the Sound vast and empty, he felt the tremor in his hands.

Just you, then? Alan said.

Me?

You want me to deny you, then.

Never, no. I'll be here for whenever you come. But opera's your work. A man can't live without work, nothing means anything without work, you know that. And your voice, it's your life.

No. He gripped Steve's head, he brought it close, he wanted his breath on him, in him. You're my life, he said.

I'll still be your life.

No, you'll be my obsession, my place I can't get to, my life I had, half a memory, half the time a dream, maybe something I'll even come to believe I imagined.

You'll make history, Alan. You'll go down—

History? What does history mean? Nothing. It doesn't mean a thing, history. Look at our people and theirs and theirs and theirs. What did they mean? What they were when alive was history. They're in us now. The rest is dead, nothing. You and I, and Elsa and the kids, we're all that matters. And you don't want that, Steve? Don't you?

Yes! *Yes!* It's all I want, but what makes you think it won't go on if you're not here? I'll be here. They will. I'll be here whenever you want me, whenever you can come. I don't care how far away you go, or where, I'll be waiting. If I never saw you again, you'd always be with me. You're in me. I couldn't ask you to sacrifice all you've worked for, nobody could. Steve's eyes went wet, his hands floundered, at the door he turned, he stood staring. I'll never leave you, he said.

Never leave me . . . Alan watched him go to his car. He could not contain. All the Sound was battering in his blood. If he could hold the sea in his arms! But he could not contain. It spilled, spilled. *I'll never leave you.*

That moment had determined his, their, life together. Or had it been the day he met Elsa in the IGA. Or the day Edge had barked and Steve had swum under and "rescued" him? Or some mysterious moment before? When *was* beginning?

So—when he came home from New York and moved back into the house and told Steve and Elsa that he had decided on a quiet life on the Island, his own place—Steve, devastated if devoted, knew he was unshakable; and if Elsa was startled to the core—she froze as if she'd stared at a Medusa—it was she who asked nothing, who, when Steve probed, even discreetly downed him: It's an enormous decision, yes, she said, but it's Alan's decision. Why do you think he doesn't know his own mind? He's the one to suffer the consequences. He must imagine what those might be. But she added, and deep concern etched her brows, her mouth, Don't you, Alan? And he was honest with her: Not all, Elsa, but I'll take them. And always after—subjected as he was to the amazement and probing of town—he was grateful: she never questioned the decision, she kept silent.

But, no fool, he would not jeopardize their lives. After some months home—discreet too and spending the usual Sundays with Steve's family—he said, I've found a small place up the road, on an inlet in Mattituck, but Elsa's going to have to see it to give it her seal of approval. Then I'll show you how I've put music into cooking.

Alone with him, Steve said, And *your* place? I'll sell it, he said. Sell it! But your life's in that house. You're my life, Alan said, and I'll be only a few minutes away. He saw how theirs would be: a "back street" life. Steve, he said, how many get to choose the life they really want?

And he went to work at his uncle's bank in Riverhead. At first he was "the one who quit opera" but soon became Peabody's nephew working at the bank.

Till now.

He hears . . . Is it Anne? Yes. And Julius. Back. He smells the fresh air whiffed in before he sees them. Dozing again. Wasting what's left. And with them right here.

Alan, Anne says, look.

Queen Anne's lace.

Julius hands him the wildflower.

Such grace! Foamy white, and all those purple centers tiny as pinheads. Pity they don't survive indoors.

My favorite! Alan says.

Julius nods. Even stooped, he seems incredibly tall, his arm wiry, his fingers cords.

In—ex—ppp—lllluh—ble, Julius says, bbb—you—y. His lips are laden with saliva.

Beauty is inexplicable. We walked the marsh. The grass is a sea of green and silver with a foam of vanilla flowers, Anne says. Ssss—par—na, Julius says. Through the Spartina grass, yes, Anne says, but we spent most of the time on a flat watching a fiddler crab work piling up mud balls underwater— *U-ca pug-nax*, Julius bursts with starting clarity—and the males wielding their big claw to seduce the females. Mir—ccculs, Julius says.

Julius himself is a miracle. How the remotest life stirs life in him! Even now, with his tongue a struggle and his limbs clumsy, his eyes prey relentlessly.

And the osprey's refurbished its nest by the marina, Anne says. The old bird's wise, it's got an open view of everything that goes on below. *That* bird's not going to starve. Anne laughs and calls out, Need any help in the kitchen? and Elsa cries, No, you entertain yourselves. And Anne says, Good. Gramp and I are into Behl's latest article on barnacles. Behl worked under Gramp.

Steve, who has gone through the Sunday paper, now and again reading Alan a few lines, lounges beside him. But Steve knows, as he does, that there is no need for talk; for years there has been little need for talk, though when there was, he, Alan, did most of the talking. Alan has learned from Julius, who has learned from infinite time and evolution and does not blind himself with the illusions of religion or history, that while the race exists what is is important and endlessly fascinating and exciting: life, any life. Alan is startled now at how, since he has lain in this chair or in his bed, he has become increasingly susceptible to silent sounds near and far, motions that would once have been unheard music, now so magnified and reverberating inside him that he feels he can touch them. Do they penetrate his skin? Or does he pass into them, carried? What he realizes is that it is passing through them too; they do not hear it yet or if they do they do not mention it either, but it is theirs too, it is what they are.

He murmurs, Swim. Steve, why don't you? It'd do you good.

You wouldn't think so to hear my breath break when I come up from under.

Magic. Nice underwater, Alan murmurs. Skates—I followed them down—so white, it was easy.

Because you're a fast one! You could live underwater. Tide's too low for skates now. You have to swim down the ledges to get anywhere, and deep.

I've seen them near shore in any tide.

The boulders are exposed. That's when you see how much life is clinging to stone below the low tidemark.

Julius flicks an enthusiastic finger: Bar—nn—les.

Cities of barnacles, Anne says. They were one of Darwin's loves.

Julius nodded vigorously. Stuh—ee. He holds up eight fingers. —earsss.

Darwin spent eight years studying those tiny creatures.

—maph—ro—

Hermaphroditic little marvels, Anne says.

And you, Anne, Alan whispers, what're you into?

Steve wants to tell Alan, Don't talk. But Elsa has said, Let him do anything he wants to. Wouldn't you want to?

Steve depends. Elsa is the keel. Without her, how to handle this, or himself?

Horseshoe crabs. In May we tagged a good number, Anne says. Someday we'll find out where they come from to mate in their couple of hours of full moon.

Ol—er dddie—nnn—srrrs, Julius says.

Imagine them being around for some 360 million years and outliving dinosaurs, Anne says.

Heavens! Elsa says. That would be too lonely, and imagine

what we'd look like! She sits beside Alan and hands him the glass as once she handed milk or orange juice to Roland or Anne. She doesn't say a word. Alan is putty in her hands, always has been. He takes the pill and drinks obediently from the glass she holds. She smiles. You'll look good with a white mustache, Alan. He too smiles and raises his hand slow as a weight to wipe his mouth clean.

Now it strikes Steve: Unconsciously Alan is the nucleus here. But hasn't he always been? Actually, in a natural way—unconscious, too—they have never been far from Alan. As kids, when Anne and Roland argued, invariably one would say I'm going to Uncle Alan's, and went, stayed overnight; older, they stayed weekends. When Roland had girl problems or Anne moped over some boy he and Elsa didn't much approve of, off to Alan they went. And Elsa had every confidence in him: Why don't you go talk it over with Alan?

Suddenly Steve wants to say, Alan, get out of that chair, let's go sailing, let's go swimming, let's go crabbing. He wants to say, Run into New York with us for the day. He wants to say, Take the ferry to New London with us. In an instant Alan will stand up, lithe, walk the beach miles with them, swim. Steve cannot imagine Alan not doing any of those things. But Alan cannot. Tomorrow. Steve cannot imagine *tomorrow.* He cannot imagine emptiness, the empty chair. Most he cannot imagine silence. He wants Alan's voice. Where is it, that wonderful rich voice? He cannot imagine opening Alan's door in Mattituck and calling out, Are you here? Where are you? and not hearing that voice. What will happen when he opens that door? Sometimes he fears Alan is right: Maybe we have imagined this life together? You can imagine anything, but imagination cannot hold onto it. It is then Steve sees *himself* in the wheelchair, he *is* Alan: He sees Steve and Elsa and Roland and Anne and Julius and would give anything if he could prevent their grief.

He knows but doesn't want to believe Alan is leaving him. Part of you is always going—in sex, work, children—diminished but extending—and with all your dead. Yes, it goes all your life little by little like something's used you. He knows: He will go out to the fields alone, he will find it there where he has always found it—at first sky, space, flat fields, and then sudden green, then green and green and green burgeoning, like growing right through his flesh.

Disease is burgeoning in Alan's flesh, it is diminishing him, replacing him. Steve came home from the fields one day to find Alan in bed here. Elsa said I went to Mattituck. I found him on the floor, moaning in pain. I wanted him to go to the hospital, but he said, No, not the hospital, to Doctor Lux. Alan never said how far advanced it was. Doctor Lux said it was Alan's choice, the hospital or home. No, I said, ours. I brought him here.

Ours.

How willingly she assumed his life: first his father, then his friend.

He had never loved her more.

Julius suddenly makes what sounds like a struggling laugh. Musing, Steve has missed the talk. Julius is beside Alan. He has been like a companion to Alan, vigilant, with his hands, eyes, and intonations speaking a private language to Alan. Now Julius raises a hand: Wait. He goes to his room and returns with the perfect carapace of a horseshoe crab from his collection. He sets it in Alan's lap. He holds up the fingers of both hands, counting: seventeen.

Anne laughs. Imagine shedding seventeen times in this life!

How do they get out without breaking the shell?

Julius flattens his palms almost together.

Anne says, They slip through a narrow slit in the front of their shell.

They're making a naturalist's textbook of you, Alan, Steve says.

Alan can barely whisper: I used to watch them copulate.

She delves into the sand and shoots her fertilized eggs in.

A little uncomfortable, that, Alan murmurs.

You and your pixie humor! Anne says.

Steve laughs. Julius's throat throttles too.

Am I missing something? Elsa crosses from the kitchen.

Alan's entertaining us.

Then I *am* missing something. Steve, set up the trays, will you?

We're all too comfortable to eat in the dining room. Everything's laid out in the kitchen. You can help yourselves. Anne, bring Dad's plate—it's ready. Alan, I've made your favorite—cream of squash.

Alan nods. His lids flutter.

Steve and Ann set up the tray tables.

Julius stands watching gulls ride the air on still wings. All the Sound and sky seem to pour in through the windows. Sun glitters on the crystal, and the flowers in the carpet seem to rise to it.

There, Dad, Elsa says, setting down Julius's prepared tray.

Julius likes the footrest. He sits beside Alan. He has learned to eat with his good left hand.

No, no, Mom, Anne says, this is my treat. You can do it anytime. Anne takes Alan's soup. Alan is groggy, his head wavering. Alan? He opens his eyes, smiles. Soup? He says nothing, smiles, gazing into her eyes as if fascinated. Steve watches, his fork gripped; he goes abruptly cold. Anne, he sees, gives her coaxing grimace: Well, I can't do it without help, and I know how you love it. And when she insists the spoon, Alan opens his mouth, then closes his eyes and nods yes, slurs, Luscious, and opens his eyes and turns them on Elsa, who says, Didn't I tell you your tastes have become my own, Alan? Though Steve catches the faintest drop in her voice, he dares not shift his glance to Elsa. He feels himself quiver. He sets his fork down. How could he handle this without her? How can she? Because she knows I'm here, he thinks, and because she loves him.

Below, the Sound seems to have heaved a sudden breath; the tide has begun to change; low, brisk waves with clean edges cut forward and break.

Elsa puts on a CD. In an instant incredibly individual notes cut the air clean and in as relentless a flow as those waves. Alan smiles, and Julius. Julius says Gggg—nnn Goooo—, though they all know Gould's is not his favorite recording of the *Variations*. They expect Alan's usual comment: True composers are higher mathematicians because they aspire to the unheard music. Bach gives us the sounds of silence. Alan doesn't say it. His fingers quiver.

Milk? Anne does not try to force him, but he nods and sips, then eases back into the sounds and closes his eyes.

Anne, as always, marvels: If I could master crust and meringue like yours, Mom.

I don't know why you can't. You've certainly got the patience, at least when it comes to creepy crawly things.

You!

Elsa laughs.

Steve is certain that if half Anne's interest in nature came from Julius, the other half was nurtured by the hours and hours she and Roland spent wading or rowing in the ponds and cricks, fishing and crabbing or scalloping, or in the woods, with Alan. Alan, the birdwatcher. You get up early enough you'll hear paradise, he'd say. Roland was lazy, but not Anne; excited, she'd be awake before Alan. With Roland avid to poke and disturb things, she'd cry, Leave it alone! She never touched. She watched and watched. She wanted to know what creatures did, how. And marveled. Life filled her life. When she came home from the university, she'd spend hours in the field with him, talking over insect problems.

Julius rises. Time for his nap. He turns a questioning face to Anne. Oh, she says, I'll be here when you come down. I'm not driving to Stony Brook until early morning.

I'm keeping her busy until then, Elsa says. Don't want her to lose touch with the mundane tasks.

Elsa catches Anne's questioning look at him, Steve, and quickly says, Into the kitchen with you, girl, and for the slightest interval Elsa's eyes linger on his, he smiles wistfully at her, and a warm flush comes over him: If you can see love, he has just seen it in that interval: what she knows, what she and he have together, love, this presence in a room.

Alan flags his hand. It is no feeble gesture, but fervent, energetic—his hand does not fall, he maintains it. Down, he whispers. Take me.

Down there? You want the beach?

Alan nods.

Steve glances at Elsa, who is startled, but still, yet nods to

Steve and says The day's right for it, hot, beautiful. What you want— I'll get a folding chair from the hall closet. Let Anne go down and set it up.

Anne returns with the chair and heads down.

Anne, wait, she says. Where, Alan?

There, near those two great boulders.

Anne descends the slope. From above they see her stretch her arms to the glory of sun, and the faintest breeze presses at her long chestnut hair. Then she calls, Ready!

Are you? Steve says to Alan.

Alan smiles. All my life, ready. It is to Elsa he says it with such a look of tenderness that she can say only, Oh, you, Alan! and turn away, Steve sees, to watch in the mirror how he carefully raises Alan from the chair—long, longer now, so much bone, skin; carries him as he once carried Roland or Anne asleep, Alan with all confidence sinking against him, his head resting against his neck.

Lord leaps up, all life now, circling, barking, his tail going, all tongue. He shoves past and heads down.

Good to feel you, Alan says, so firm. Steve is startled at how feverish Alan's hand is. Dry too his forehead.

The tide is out so the undersides of the boulders are exposed, green and dark with algae and seaweed like the shoreline. Along the sand, below the width of pure white stones, there is a thick neat line of dead moths, thousands after thousands, washed up and deposited all along the beach. Yesterday, their one day to breed, all the trees, all the air palpitated with their white wings. Last night they'd all sat out back, watching the woods breathe white. Magic. A miracle. Then nothing. Steve does not want to believe, like Alan, that it is all a meaningless groping against nothing. He marvels. Perhaps that is his father's influence and his daughter's, because he is moved by Julius's and Anne's constant awe before what it is in anything that struggles against such impossible odds and leaves something to stand against nothing. Did she and Dad see the ridge of moths in their meanderings this morning? And he—he can't define it, wouldn't—he is magnetized by the land, loves it, something insistent in a green shoot, a sudden furrow of life, stirs as if it is germinating in his own body.

Alan murmurs You're not going in?

But—

I want to see you swim.

Steve doesn't want to budge, not for a minute. He wants Alan's breath, his motions, his words; he fears not to be near; he's afraid to leave because he feels he would be leaving his own breath and motion, bereft—bereft. I don't want to be denied anything, no matter what, he tells himself.

No buts. But Alan coughs and, after, whispers, I'll be watching you every second. Like a fish, you, Alan whispers, his teeth the old full smile.

Proud Alan looks. Of me. He always was.

You're sure?

When more? I said I want to see you. He whispers soft, You fool, Steve.

At the water's edge Steve glances back, and waves to them up there, then calls to Alan, Here goes. Alan raises an arm to him. Steve takes a running dive in deep, emerges, and swims, swims vigorously: He goes under, he sees a white body, he touches flesh, grips that body, hauls it up, breaks the surface, and sees the dog: but no—not Edge, not black, not barking. Edge. Did he imagine? No. Alan is there. But Lord. The house. All the fields beyond. This life. How did it come about, this life? It frightens him to think how that day he might have missed the dog by a second, he might have turned up the sand toward the fresh water pond below the woods, he might have halted in his walk along the beach and turned back, he might have ignored the barking and all his life been changed: no Alan up there, not that house, not twenty-five years of . . . Gone. This moment he can believe he has imagined the trip from Brooklyn to Alan's apartment in New York, imagined all the years back and forth to the cottage in Mattituck, all the Sundays of their lives here, the days he glimpsed Alan in the bank, and always—the miracle—Elsa and Alan cronies, as if *they* were the lovers, as if *he*, then, were the mate. Nothing startled him and Elsa more than the day Alan said it was foolish to hang on to an empty furnished house and let it go to ruin and it would be blasphemous to rent the family place, so he'd put it up for sale though he'd hate to cut that old life off. Steve himself brooded, and Elsa—not only because Alan would no longer be a stone's throw from them, but because the house too was Alan, the house had become their world too, home. After that house open to sea, deep in sky, in their own house in town, so surrounded, they felt confined. And it was Elsa who read his mind—when hadn't she?—and said We can't afford to lose this chance, Steve, let's buy the Peabody house, I've dreamed of living in it: meaning too, he knew, You want it, don't you? as if none of them could break up the life in that house. Did Elsa know what she was doing? Elsa arranged the surprise with Ed Stockton, who called Alan to say he had a buyer. When Alan showed up at the realty office, bewildered at sight of her and Steve, Elsa said, We're selling our house too; but seeing Alan go pale, she laughed and said, Tell him, Ed, and Ed let it out: They're buying your place, Alan. Alan turned stone an instant. He stared at Elsa, at Steve. His eyes went wet. You! She took his hand. I knew you'd be glad it was in the right hands.

So Alan left but did not leave. Sundays and at random moments he came "home" to them. And in a strange way, once in the house, Steve, standing in a north window staring over the Sound toward the Connecticut shore, more and more came to realize I am Alan.

Nights in Mattituck, sometimes Alan cooked—for four, for bridge, with the occasional social fourth who never amounted to anything more. But it was the children Alan wanted, and they wanted him—and more and more as they grew it was an incessant cry, Can we spend the weekend in Mattituck with Uncle Alan? And, soon old enough, they had their own rowboat there at his little pier; they could row, swim, fish on their own.

They might as well be yours, Alan, Elsa said.

And they *are*, Steve thinks now, they are. Hasn't he passed through my body into hers. Wasn't his mouth on me, his hands, and his cock in me. He's held me, so held her. And all the years when she's held me after, hasn't she held him in her arms too? And didn't

I take her to him? So how can the children *not* be his too, or we not be his, or he not be ours.

Now he goes under again, but thrusts himself quickly up, bursts into the bold sun, a blinding white sheet over the water. Alan? But of course he's still there! Voices carry over the surface. Julius and Anne. Elsa appears in the doorway an instant. Checking on Alan. She'll be devastated. She hardly sleeps. She's like a quiet phantom hovering constantly, vigilant but as unobtrusive as possible. Vigilant over him too. But he fears for her: Alan has been her friend, her confessor in everything—in almost everything? Yesterday—wasn't it? how could it be years?—while he insisted on working the fields, it was Alan who took time off once Elsa had the babies, watched over her, ran errands, helped feed them, burp them, put them to sleep; who came away smelling of Johnson's baby powder or sour burp. Why *wouldn't* they be his children! So, coming in from the fields, he half the time expected to hear their voices, Elsa's and Alan's, talking and laughing sometimes like children themselves, siblings.

How lost she'd be!

Nobody could have adjusted more—why had she?—though his love for her never for one instant flagged, as Alan knew, as she surely knew, for his desire for her never languished; if anything it grew more vital, yes, as she surely knew, which meant that there was a fullness in his love, mind and body: as she knew too, yes—how could she not?—because she maddened the man in him as he did the man in Alan, a needed part of his own nature that in no way diminished his love or desire for her, which more existed when Alan roused sensations in him similar to her own, which she experienced only with him, Steve. At moments with Alan, then, he understood something of Elsa he might never have understood without Alan: With Alan he was as near to experiencing her sexual experience with him as he would ever be. And it made him love her—and Alan—more.

And her them—if she knew.

And she must know, yes, but would never—never did—speak: except implicitly. Yes, but once only:

When the roof to Alan's house in Mattituck leaked.

He told Alan, It needs a whole new roof. Go to Wilson's. Pat'll send somebody out to tell you what you need. I can put it on in no time.

At supper that night he told Elsa, Our house needs a roof.

When he looked up, she was staring across the kitchen—at nothing. In the act he realized it: *our*.

But she sat, steady.

Roof? she said.

Yes. It's leaking. If I don't do it now, the rain will wreck his ceilings. Good thing it's my slack time, and it'll keep Tanner busy, he's a good man, I like to keep him on year round.

And how long will it take?

Several days, probably a week.

I see.

Whatever she saw, she took with her. In the morning she said This is Anne's last year before starting school, the kids better see their grandparents while there's time. Since you'll be working on the roof, this is a good week for a visit. . . .

But I could go with you. I can always do the roof. I don't have to do it now.

You don't have to do anything, she said, do you?

He worked feverishly all week to drive out the agony of thinking, waiting, feeling his thoughts corrode because he mentioned nothing—what could he mention?—to Alan, who, silent too, he knew harbored his own suspicions.

She came home tranquil, relieved to be back, *released into my own kitchen*, and she really burgeoned when—he knew something then— in a move almost any other woman would call ridiculous, sacrificial, even perverse: The first thing she did was to call Alan and say the kids couldn't wait to see him; and suppertime he came and slumped onto the floor for games with them and they ended up screaming and laughing with him as usual. And for a moment Steve thought, She's found a way, it's Alan, it's a game for life she's decided to play; and only for an instant thought, But it could have happened, been happening, been going on for years; thought, I don't believe—; thought, Why wouldn't she?; thought, And if it had happened, did, would happen . . .?; thought, You're thinking what she must have thought, what she's thinking; thought, But she's back here with us, with me, mine, she's thought something out, she's made a decision, she's hasn't said a thing, she may never, and *that* says everything; and he was ashamed, ashamed of what he was thinking, assuming, condemning when there was no reason, no *what* to condemn in her or ultimately for her to condemn in him, despite his love for Alan, for he knew she must know he could not live without her, did not want to, ever; and ultimately there was nothing to condemn in Alan either because Alan loved her too and now as he watched them together, he was ashamed not at what was possible between them, bed, sex, but what he was thinking without cause—because he could bear it *with* cause, yes, if she ever showed that: He saw in her silence how much she loved Alan too, what he meant to her, some *too much* that she must have decided she could not give up, that would deplete her life too much as it would his, *because* it would his, and Alan's.

Now he hurries across the sand, as if running from the moment of that barking, the black dog, Edge, the resonant voice, the touch of that body he dived into these waters to rescue and held, running through years till he is running toward his own dog, Lord, moaning by Alan's chair, toward this Alan he must be imagining, this long body shrunken to bone, sharp angles he is almost afraid to lift for fear of breaking bones, and that face long because so sunken, but still the rich sandy hair, thicker it seems now falling so youthfully over his hung head.

Alan! he calls. . . .

Alan, Elsa murmurs in her kitchen as so many times, years of times, she has said it to him straddling a chair beside her; but now she whispers What is this that you, I, we have made? Her thought fragments. She cannot decide what it is she is asking. I sound like Dad, she thinks, sadly ironical.

Not to feign casual, but not to alarm, she moves past Julius's room. The door is open. He is reading but looks up. She says, An after-dinner cordial, Dad? Though usually impervious to sounds and interruptions, he is distracted; and, unusual too, nods and says, —esss, so she goes on to the kitchen and pours him an Amoretto and takes it to him. She cannot decide what it was she was trying to ask . . . of Alan? herself? . . . when she hears Anne slide the door open and close it and cross the living room.

How Alan loves the Sound! I was sure he'd get up and walk. It's unbelievable. A rush of color came into his face. He broke into talk. You'd think— It startled Dad, or scared him. I couldn't tell.

They're—he's—always at home down there.

All Dad's great experiences, he's told me, have happened on the Sound, though which he must feel too sacred to tell.

There's always a limit, even between the most intimate. And that's no bad thing. There's always—should be—that last respect: there's something sacred about that, even when you know, if you can, all you could reduce knowing to—

You're talking like a biologist now. Even when you know and want to save—as we do, Gramp and I, for instance—there's a respect for what we don't, or can't, know—the *why*, not just the *how*, of what things do—it's there the respect comes, even for the most malignant things in the universe.

Malignant?

I mean what wants to live, innocently, at the expense of our or other bodies. Only that.

That's a pretty big only.

I'm afraid we're all merely onlys, but each loves his own life enough not to want to lose it no matter what the consequences. I wonder what we'd do without those malignant creatures to challenge us to keep life going.

Going, Elsa thinks. Once she wanted it—for one insane instant—to stop. He had come back, Steve, from the City with a quiet serenity so isolating, so inviolable, at the same time tender, a quiet flame she could warm at but not touch without a fearful wondering; and close—that was the night—she had smelled (she had never felt more animal) the alien smell: It was on him, it pervaded his skin, hair, his lips, strong on his hands, as if no washing could remove it. . . .

Going, Elsa says.

Of course. Because it can't stop. Nothing can stop it. Living by the sea, every minute you see that: the waves, the shells, and dead fish, but always something emerging, fiddler crabs, starfish, and between refuse tossed up and all the life there, beach roses and sandfleas and . . . .

But things do stop. People stop things.

Anne says nothing for a moment. Their own things, then, she says, but not themselves, unless unnaturally.

Alan did.

Stop?

Stop singing.

But not whatever went on in him. Perhaps he transferred it.

Or, Elsa thinks, discovered the one true music. Once she was sure Alan in an instant had taken hers, taken it away from her forever. It had gone to the Peabody house—in Steve, through Steve, with Steve. How could she have said it then? She couldn't say it, said nothing: at Steve's madness.

Nights she'd thought I'll go to Alan? I'll confront Steve? I'll corner them when alone, talking their—intimacies? Do they? What? How?

But refrained.

What held her back? What in her kept her from it? It wasn't that she couldn't believe it possible—of Alan, of Steve. No blind fury, no impulse to rage at her intimate loss, not How could Alan take mine? What's mine? It was not discretion, but confusion, yes, a gut-scraping desire to know, know what exactly to reason with, which required what she had never asked before, never, *who we are, what, what we are doing together* because . . . because any move, she pondered, would disturb so that the very air they breathed, would change and all tranquillity, every sense of union between them, her and them, them and the children, would turn as turbulent as a sudden whipping of a silt deep in the three of them that muddied and blinded so that—she saw it, but inexplicably, or inexplicably at that moment—she had to wait, have patience, to *see*.

Look at this, Ann says, a trail of ants.

You can't keep them out. Steve will have to use some sealant.

It was, Elsa thinks, that *I* could not give Alan up either. Either? Would Steve have? Or wouldn't I face that question? Anyway, I didn't. Maybe not facing it was facing it. I chose that.

I'll spray, Anne says, though Elsa knows how Anne hates to kill. It's contrary to all her work and the beliefs behind it, and Julius's. Anne loves him—her worry, Julius—more even than she loves the others because Julius, Anne always unselfishly maintains, her bible until her own research, has made her the naturalist she is. Like collaborators they are now; so most weekends she's home—for Julius, yes, or is she too disguising what she feels for Alan?

I'll wash the dishes off, Anne. You put them in the washer.

When the washer begins its strike of spray, Anne says, I can't imagine what Dad will do if—

When, Elsa says.

Burying his, our, own life, a part, intimate. It dies forever.

It will seem strange coming home, or going to Mattituck, without—

Elsa says—she wants to believe it—People are in the things they had. You touch them there.

It's not the same.

Of course not, but after a while it turns grief into a pleasant memory, or how explain how the past memory turns us suddenly happy at certain moments? And you can always call up memories to console you.

Won't we be like aliens in Alan's house? In a way it's always been his.

Always.

Does it ever strike you that we took it over?

Elsa smiles. Invaders? And thinks, Not *here* took over, but somewhere—New York City?—was the real invasion. But whose was it? Alan's? Steve's? It doesn't matter now. It happened. That's everything.

Yes, invaders, but not any old Snopeses, but good, innocent people. We are.

And suddenly Anne turns and kisses her on the cheek, holds her close and tight—so unlike Anne, her detached daughter, more like Roland this instant.

What will you do, Mom?"

Me?

But, if she concealed it well, if in clinging an instant to Anne and then holding herself off, startled to wonder not only what Anne knew or thought but perhaps even for how long, because children absorb, intuit, feel years before articulating, when they do, what they have been intuiting all along; and Anne and Roland had lived so long with their lives that what, articulated, might have seemed unnatural to them had become natural over the years. And who could love them more than Alan does? Or they him?

Do? she says. Live without, as your father will, hard as that may be.

Saying it, she feels a current of fear—at change; feels nothing remotely—blasphemously—like a selfish thought or a fear of some old restoration of two alone: She cannot only not think that, but cannot imagine that now, the two alone, without lament.

But at Anne's question—What will you do?—she sees Anne sees, or feels. Her eyes fill at some unspoken understanding latent in Anne's question.

That Anne has asked indicates both knowledge and concern at their loss—of whatever kind—because Anne is aware of what she's losing, as Roland is though not here. And what would *Anne* do, or Roland? For how after all the years mention *Dad* without *and Alan*, true paternal love? So why now? How could Elsa possibly be startled *except* by the articulation, if allusive, of what their, *our*, relationships are, she thinks with a tremor, reverberating already with the momentary absence of Alan and Steve in the house, with even Julius's quiet, with only Anne's breathing, repressed too at this moment as she lets her go and says, It will cost all God knows what wrenching to adjust our lives.

And you most—

Me?

Because you bear most.

Elsa catches the soft intimacy in Anne, but must defend:

We don't know what men bear. Most men don't talk much. Think what Alan's going through, what he's leaving . . . Elsa is thinking, Leaving Steve and me and you and Roland and Julius—but says, What he's lived for, lives for . . . Her voice clouds.

At this instant Alan is a presence almost palpable. All the years he has been almost palpable; she has never dwelled long on imagining, trying to visualize them lying together—Alan and Steve, her and Alan—because, she realizes, he so gradually came to be a presence, invisible, at first intrusive, confusing, even confounding her, but soon a visible, strange comfort, then a constancy, a companion missed and then desired, sought, till he was *home* itself, close. . . . Alan was so close she was held in his smell, she touched his smell, knew it was his skin on Steve, his sweat, his semen—sometimes in that momentary ecstasy of oblivion with Steve sure that what had passed into Steve was passing into her, for how through years could she separate the two, without having Alan having him, and as comforter more: because Steve, so silent, left talk to Alan, no husband yet husband, by law and rite nothing, by proximity and habit virtually everything.

Nobody knows, Elsa says, what his sacrifice cost.

Anne appears struck—Not you?—and looks straight at her, into.

Elsa does not betray, but sustains, her gaze. She does not reply. She is struggling with herself, clumsily, to define something she feels: if even silently she could articulate it now to Alan—some word to pass into air to him, some telepathic communication, some expression of a self that has never in any way spoken, dared to speak, of what *he* gave up, and gave, and made her an ambiguous and then willing partner to, bound.

Alan! Oh, Alan! She feels helpless to tell. What you tell never *says*! A quick fire of unspoken words tears through her, making her hands want to speak, and her eyes. Oh, why are you so helpless to tell! If she could find the word and murmur it, he would hear and know. But what word for all this?

Abruptly she murmurs, Anne, Julius is alone. Perhaps he'd

like to sit with us. Ask him, will you? Anne goes in hurry, as if impelled by her urgency.

In a few moments she returns with Julius, Julius this comfort, if stoic, *because* stoic, with the warm gaze, always grateful for *now*.

Julius, she murmurs helplessly. Anne, she murmurs helplessly.

She can find no word, but stares in wonder at this sudden perception of the three, an image as palpable as Anne, as Julius standing there: She sees herself a girl sitting in the middle of a seesaw while Steve and Alan ride up/down, up/down, and then balance, balance perfectly still; then one falls, one end falls, the seesaw shoots up . . . .

Alan! Oh, through all the years what without you would our marriage have been? What?

A piercing howl breaks from the beach. What . . .?

Lord? That's Lord!

And before Anne and Julius respond, she presses to the window. She looks down by the great boulders:

Steve is just coming out of the waves, laughing, both hands whipping water from his face. The dog is howling. For an instant Steve does not move, then breaks and comes up before Alan and falls to his knees. Alan is slumped into a knot in his chair. Steve raises Alan's head, he talks to Alan, he clutches Alan's head close, then his face seems to crack, he lets Alan's head fall, his head hangs. Steve pounds the sand furiously, heaving great broken cries.

Alan! Elsa cries.

Mom? Anne says.

Call Doctor Lux, Elsa says.

Oh, Julius, she murmurs.

Julius's mouth moves but makes no sound.

I'm going down to them, Elsa says.

Lord howls.

WATCHING MARIE

It was the hottest July. The church was stifling, but when the choir came singing in, led by James Dickinson Manfred Verity, you forgot the heat. Something of the sonorous elegance of his name heralded Dick's presence. It was a joyful startle to behold him in his red robe, a form and a face any man might envy, followed by his two robust brothers, handsome too, and the paired singers. His rotund baritone was the keel to the choir, which floundered somewhat when he or the brothers were absent; and his absence seemed to diminish even Reverend Barton's faith and tarnish his sermon. But this day, in the wake of the Fourth, with so many visitors in town, the service was crowded, the choir full and inspired, and the minister radiant at such plenitude. After the benediction, as he surveyed the audience with an almost paternal pleasure, his gaze dropped and rested for an almost imperceptible second on a front pew, where at just that moment a head tilted noticeably sideways and light caught from the stained glass windows made the honey hair glow like an instant star. My heart leaped.

Marie was back.

She would not stop coming back for years despite that summer. She would come back even after all her girlhood friends had married and dispersed, after many of their parents had died, and for years after what my grandmother had called the "lamentable degradation" of her sons, by which, if she meant all three of them, she really had Dick in mind. Marie would simply arrive at The Hall as she had arrived unexpectedly since the year she went off to the

Sorbonne. She would appear from Paris or Madrid or London—or New York, where she would be photographed for the magazine covers, which her beautiful head occasionally graced. As if she had to renew herself at the fount, she appeared like a strange migrating bird, and as much under the sway of natural forces, though only she knew the appointed day.

Marie was anybody's cameo. In repose her beauty reflected a Grace Kelly serenity, and in motion the innocent spontaneity of an Audrey Hepburn; but, romantic and sensitive and impressionable as I was, in some intuitive way, perhaps as a reflection of my own passion, a melodramatic passion at that, I knew—knew—that behind that facade a like passion smoldered. And when she had become a world-traveled student and model and could sit poised for long periods as if frozen motionless, I knew that her poise was also useful in concealing that passion.

As a very young boy I waited and watched for Marie all through my summer visits to my grandparents. She and my two aunts, one a year older, the other a year younger than Marie, had been in high school at the same time and inseparable. And I waited through the years when she came home from the Sorbonne and later when as the famous model she came from whatever foreign city, though mostly from Paris—she had long since bought the chalet at Seine-et-Oise. I would watch her when she was with my aunts. Sometimes lying in the field or against a tree across the road from The Hall, I would watch for her.

The Hall was outside the village, on the cliff overlooking the Sound. Close, from the road you could catch glimpses though the bushes, but far off you viewed its full, simple majesty. Two-story granite, harsh, unadorned, with a simple Georgian harmony, The Hall had a proud, defiant look. In storm, when rain and wind battered the house and bent trees and flattened bushes, my soul exulted. The Hall was Wuthering Heights. I was Heathcliff, the wretched orphan doomed to walk the earth exiled from my Catherine. More, I was the storm, doomed to run itself out and Wuthering Heights to stand strong against it.

That Sunday, waiting outside the church, I carried the storm too. Marie was of course surrounded, and in no time my aunt Alice and then Hazel were laughing as if yesterday, and my uncles came out and Marie opened her arms to them, all three—and then she caught sight of me. Something halted her, there was a brief interval of staring, then the recognition. "Why, it's Hal." She came to me and again her gaze lingered on my face. "How you've matured! Why, you could be—" She smiled and then her cheek brushed mine. I was afraid she would feel me trembling. I thought I was over the days when I would retreat to the bathroom and, trembling as I tempted myself, close my eyes so as not to sully the purity of Marie's image. Perhaps, I thought after she'd gone, she was arrested by my dark hair—for she wasn't the only one— which when dry hung loose in two waves over my forehead like Dick's: We were the only two dark-haired ones in a family of strawberry blondes and I too had the Verity nose, but the full red lips were my father's.

Though she would see me often enough after, Marie would not look at me again with such scrutiny for years and then it would be for the last time.

There was a year or two between my uncles—that summer they were in their thirties, still the most attractive and eligible bachelors in town, always dating but—incomprehensibly—slow to marry. Perhaps the boys were waiting for Dick to take the lead; but Dick, always in demand, was leading the high life. To see him in white ducks and a blazer and straw hat, in the most quietly elegant summer wear, sometimes even sporting a cane, or in casual yachting clothes, one might see why he was called The Duke of Greenport. And he could talk—an easy, flowing rhetoric in a rich, binding voice. Unintentionally he lured women and charmed men, the rich and cultured and famous, despite his work—for with Ralph and Jared he was an oysterman and fisherman and sometimes house painter—and evenings and weekends he'd be at this or that summer guest's or dining at Mitchell's or fishing from those imperial yachts that docked at Preston's for the season, and nobody at home ever knew where Dick was or when he'd be back, all of which meant to the family that he "had possibilities."

They imagined him in some kind of future glory quite removed from them. Still, in my reserve—quietly removed from the family as I was—I saw that despite his gifts Dick wasn't quite the authentic article: You had only to observe the others' delicate hands, their casual speech, the ease of postures almost inherited by generations of comfort, and the always friendly but reserved eye with which they viewed the world. And Dick—nobody's fool—surely was aware that that was why he had to exert himself with as much casual ease as he could muster to maintain an apparent comfort, a "genuine" ease with them.

Except for the few exploits, which Dick shared with the family, the only high life at my grandmother's house was Marie. Whenever she was there, the atmosphere was transformed. If, finely dressed and refined, she brought The Hall in, she was soon beating potatoes or rolling dough with Alice and Hazel, all three talking up a storm, filling the house with laughter as always, sometimes abruptly whispering secrets or after supper retiring and playing cards with my uncles. Until she went abroad she was day and night with the girls—at carnivals and circuses and movies and art shows on the docks and at the firemen's fair and St. Mary's bazaar and ice skating in winter or roller skating in summer at the Legion hall rink, and at all the church affairs, and swimming and picnicking . . . . So it was natural that to the family and all the town she was like one sister more; and it was as natural for her to join any sailing or fishing party headed off Montauk with Dick or Paul or Jared as guide or guest, or to appear at any elite affair at which Dick was also present, and it might have been as natural to see her alone anywhere with one of my uncles though her social discretion must always have kept her from that.

By that summer she had been for some years the famous model; my uncle Paul and I had been to "Hitler's war," as the family called it; as a medic Paul had survived the war only to have drowned with his childhood buddy Freddy Latham in a sudden storm off Plum Island while trying out a rowboat they had built; and I was studying for an advanced degree in literature. Dick had not been called and Jared had been sent to reform school for some mystery the family would never divulge and later at induction had faked his health. When I learned Marie was just back from Rome, I couldn't wait to corner her—and I did two days after church, at the beach, where I knew she'd be swimming with my aunts; married now, they still made plenty of time for Marie. I drove to the Sound beach, parked—spotted Marie immediately among bikinis and two-piece suits, distinguished in the only one-piece black suit—and then planked myself down beside them, expecting and very aware of Marie's almost unobtrusive scrutiny. "Come on," I said. "I dare you—all of you—a race out to the raft." Marie rose. "You're on," she said and in an instant we took running dives into the waves. She had "prowess," I said. "No. Practice," she said as I came up after her. In no time we were sitting on the raft and as quickly we were in Rome. I took her down my great moments—standing in the Coliseum stunned by the past so alive in my eyes, descending into the dark world of the dead in the Catacombs, reciting poetry at the Fountain of Trevi—"Yes! Yes!" She knew all of it. "But *when?*" she said. "During the war, before we invaded southern France from Italy," I said, "when we lived in tents on the beach just below Civitavecchia and visited Tarquinia and the Etruscan ruins and lay in the sun on the black sand of the Tyrrhenian Sea and swam and dreamed—until the rains flooded us out. In a war you have more time to think than anything else." "And what did you dream of?" I looked long at her. I said, "Oh, you don't tell dreams." And she said, "It's best not to." "But," I said, "in Rome my most solemn and moving moment came in the Pantheon when I stood alone in that dark tomb in a shaft of light coming down from the opening in the dome, feeling separated from a love as if I actually were a character in a novel by Hawthorne and had been there before." I didn't know then that we are many people before we die. "Why, you're a romantic!" "And you're not?" She raised her fine profile and stared across the Sound at the thin line of Connecticut shore. "Shall we go in now?" she said and dived under.

Before the afternoon was over, Marie had invited me to stop by The Hall the next day for coffee or a drink—for more Rome,

I knew, and other travel and some music and literature. I exulted, of course. After all, her visitors were usually a host of outsiders—elite, we thought them; and her parents had their own limited circle from town. She presented me—"Edith Verity's son, here for the summer"—but it was the "from Yale" which caused them to linger a moment and me to smile at their consequent courtesy. Then they left us and she invited me up to her own sitter on the second floor from which we could see over the bluff to the Sound and the far shore. And, as was inevitable, we came to "where we were going" in this world. "No matter where," I said, "you get bogged down on the way—right now, it's study. And for you?" "Oh, I dream of getting bogged down." She laughed and added, "So we're back to dreams." "And you have one too?" I couldn't imagine her having one she couldn't actually live. "Too? *You're* very revealing." This time I laughed, but said, "Do you?" "Oh, mine's so common as to be laughable: to have the right person and marry and live in this town, always." That shocked: I thought, But Paris, London, Rome, Madrid, Buenos Aires . . . and at the same time thought I could want that and *now*, here, with all my future in this room, and said too quickly, "But surely you could have—," and caught myself. She smiled. "My pick?" she said. "People always say that. But nobody has her pick. Love happens. You're doomed to it." "And you're doomed to this town. Is that why you come back so insistently?" Later—in my addiction to reliving every scene with Marie—I remembered the startled flick of her eyes at my *insistently*. Then she said, "But it's my home"; and as if skirting dangerous shallows, she veered the conversation, not realizing that the shallows, for me, were equally dangerous. "And you—you're doomed to someone?" "Oh, yes—but . . . irremediably." "And . . .?" she said. I laughed. "To Milton and Shakespeare," I said. "You!" And we both laughed. Nonetheless, that afternoon, walking home, was the nearest I had ever come to levitation.

But I was in for a fall. Evidently we all were. My grandmother, whom the family always considered "high and mighty," couldn't stand the Polacks, though she was always courteous to them as she was kind to any "soul" in need. For some time before Marie's return, Dick and his lifelong friend Lonnie Carr had been double-dating Polish sisters from Orient—"running around with Polacks," my grandmother said, though the rest of the family took it as merely one more of Dick's womanizings, for in their vanity over Dick's good looks, they thought *Who* could resist him? So it was a shock with no relief in its reverberations when late in July Dick announced that he would marry Netta Renkowski in September at a double ceremony with Lonnie Carr and Netta's sister Rolla. "A Polack!" My grandmother cried doom. But Dick, as always, was impervious to criticism, though apart from sweet seductive smiles and very rich hair the sisters had few attractions, unless hidden ones: They were short, bordering on pudgy, with something of a peasant robustness, though they were careful in their dating dress, with high heels and evanescent dresses and wide picture hats, which created a certain ephemeral quality about them. But—the devastation—they had emphatic accents and sounded as if they were translating into English with a host of subjunctives, *when Dick be*, and omitted articles, *I go to store*.

So Dick had fallen—but no one knew yet how far. Or why.

My grandfather's brother Gill was the caretaker of a small house on a knob of land that jutted into the harbor. In plain sight from the water, it was cut off from the road by a field of reeds almost twice as tall as a man, which lined the winding driveway. The rich owner hadn't come to town in years so Gill had the house to himself. Gill was a picaro, a charming old devil who loved his booze and lived it up, especially weekends, with the known carousers, mostly younger, and who never failed to have a woman or two, invariably young, from New York for a bout. He was a red-faced laughing lover, who squinted with half-blind albino eyes through thick glasses, but so much fun and laughter and touching and rousing that the most unyielding finally gave way to his lures—or to the boys'. So it was natural that, Dick having announced the great event, Gill, who hardly needed an excuse for a celebration, seized the opportunity for Dick and Lonnie to celebrate their "lasts"; and Dick and Lonnie, who had already—so the stories went—enjoyed with the sisters the fruits of marriage on the beach, in the woods, in the back seats of cars and elsewhere, welcomed the pre-nuptial variety. Among relatives and close friends the three-day orgy was scandalous and legendary. Gill came under fire, but fortunately at the time, under the guise of owner of the house and the knob of land, he was courting a widow who had her own home in New London, and to escape the flack he took the ferry to the woman he would seduce into a marriage that would end in divorce a few months later when she found out his deceptions. So after the orgy, to let peace descend, Gill left the key with Dick "to keep an eye out."

In a town by the sea—and this one is a tiny peninsula—the sea is a companion complex and contradictory whose moods reflect your own and govern much of your life. It may console one day and turn on you the next, but the fascinations of the sea and the shore are endless, and walking the beach here is no mere tourist pastime, but the unconscious submergence in a primordial world with no time where you are moving with the same anonymous motion as a fiddler crab or starfish or sand flea or skate or horsefly or the waves and the wind. And it would be no surprise and little curiosity to see anyone walking the shore of the Sound or the bay or Sandy Beach. But it was a surprise to me one early evening when, having dropped in on Dick after a swim, I had just left Gill's place and was walking the long meandering driveway when I saw Marie walking with what looked like a deliberated athletic pace, the slight breeze riding her loose hair back and pressing her slight dress revealingly against her. She did not see me, and something of her intent look made me duck deep into the reeds. She turned into the drive and followed one of the deep ruts, passing within a few feet of me. I caught a glimpse of her face, serious—even, I thought, worried or angry. At the edge of the clearing she stopped, probably because she came upon Gill's dirty old nanny, who had as usual got her chain wound too tightly around the metal stake so couldn't menace her. It was an ugly, smelly creature whose milk Gill may have liked though I suspect he was really endeared to the dirty thing. Ever after that moment, the goat would come to mind whenever I thought of Dick's marriage and my grandmother's word *degradation.* I watched long enough to give Marie time to reach the clearing and, still hidden in the reeds, wound my way close. She crossed straight to the back door—the front faced the hospital and the houses on the bank across the water, all very close by, and of course anything that happened on that enormous lawn so meticulously kept by Gill was plainly visible from the other side. Something like shame came over me at even the thought of anything like stealth connected with Marie. I was trembling. I heard her call "Anybody in?" And in no time Dick appeared at the screen door. He looked neither surprised nor pleased—and that surprised *me*—though I sensed an air of reluctance in the deliberated slowness with which after a few murmured words he held the door open for her. I stood still as if frozen in the reeds, numbed, dumb, belying the fire in me and my seething curiosity. I could now and then hear voices but not one clear word. What could I do? I had no right to know, but had to, had to, do something.

I knew Gill's house inside and hoped they were in the front room; if so, I was safe since only the windows of the bathroom and the bedrooms on either end gave onto the rear. I crossed the lawn with enough presence to walk slowly so that should I be spotted my wandering would seem casual, and sought refuge between the windows. There was breeze enough to now and again flutter the curtains against the screen. I listened—easy because the sounds were far—occasional gulls' cries, the buzz of a motorboat, children's yells from the beach; but for a while there was only the vagueness of their voices. Of a sudden from the bedroom came Marie's voice, loud: "I gave you every chance. I did. I wouldn't have had it different. And I don't know, I still don't understand—" "Won't understand!" Dick interrupted.. "—how you could refuse all those years." "But you do know. You've known from the beginning—and every possible reason. I can't even make up another." Dick's voice was too husky, dragged. "Won't!" It came like a little vindictive cry. "Have it your way, Marie. Won't, then." "But you're not there yet, no, not . . . yet." And as much time as it took to say those words and utter a strange animal cry of confused pain and pleasure, there came the kiss and suck of lips, of clothes chafed and removed, the bed besieged, and the incessant strains and struggles and susurrations—I could have died, died with them into that, my blood near to bursting, my temple so pulsing that I could hardly think—and then the culmination in the omygodjesus gasps and cries, the bitten air, of both of them; and then, some time after, a long wail and Marie crying and then saying with such a futile sound, "You, you, oh *you*, Dick!" and he implacably, "Now, Marie, Marie. Don't, Marie. Don't make things worse. Don't, please—" and her retort, "But how could they be. How could they!"

That was the first evidence I had of what my grandmother called Dick's degradation, though for me at that moment it was what would have been inadmissible had I not seen and heard but been told it, Marie's degradation as well as Dick's. But if, tense and listening, I was stunned to such stillness that my body ached with that immobility, my thoughts ran unceasingly: How many times? Where? When had it begun? How could I, who had watched Marie for so long, have missed it? And if I was confused, turbulent, I nonetheless had enough presence to know I was menaced by the silence that followed and had to break before Marie or both came out and discovered me standing like a waiting thief. I *was* a thief. I was invading. I was stealing her secret, theirs. I broke out of that frozen stillness. If only I were invisible! I ran for the reeds. I wanted to keep running, to run and run till I had outrun even the memory of Marie, yet at the same time I wanted to see her, had to see her, to see her face, to see what the moment had done to her, to hold that sight forever, as if *I* had lost her irrecoverably—and *hadn't* I? hadn't I?—for she was in some way mine. Hadn't I, since before thought, felt she was mine? No, I couldn't tear myself away. I waited in the reeds for some time. I would have given anything to hear what they were saying, what they had said that led up to that moment in the bedroom, what history buttressed those words most of which, except for the impending but unmentioned wedding, told me little.

Finally she came to the back door. I could see her standing inside the screen door, still, long, apparently saying nothing. Then she flung it open and—her head high, her gaze lost somewhere ahead—she walked straight across the lawn past the goat to the crude dirt road with the clumps of grass grown down its middle. I heard her legs flick the grass not far from me.

But Dick very soon *was* "there." On a clear blue day—surely too painfully beautiful a day to Marie and my grandmother—Lonnie Carr and Dick and the sisters took their vows there where for years he had led the choir in singing. But no more—the Sunday before was his last appearance with the Episcopal church choir, lamentably the last of "the Verity boys" to sing with them, for Jared had recently married a Catholic. At the double wedding, the sisters' twin wedding, I waited outside—watched—for Marie, certain she would not show up—one of my foolish underestimations of her poise—until just a few minutes before the wedding she parked her little white sports car. So as not to face her, I went in quickly and stood behind the congregation. Dressed as completely in white as any bride, sleek, with long gloves and a trim little hat—her hair was drawn severely back and woven into a tight bun—and the slightest half-veil almost to the level of her eyes, she took her seat in her family pew down front—hers happened to be the groom's side—two rows behind the two where my grandparents and Jared and Alice and Hazel and their mates were sitting. As she walked down the aisle, she might have been the unexpected bride come from nowhere to claim her place—and she *was*, though I did not know yet *what* bride she was, *what* she would be married to, nor did I know that it would be a marriage for life. Watching Marie, I missed most of the details of the wedding. Dignified, she sat without stirring, rejecting, so it seemed, any trace of emotional involvement in the ceremony, for as usual at weddings women's breaths caught and there were tears no doubt evoking memories of their own moment of illusory perfection and subsequent changes and losses and what substance remained.

After, she was waylaid inside the church and talked for some time—fortunately, because she might have overshadowed the wedding, her presence alone could do that—and she went outside in time to see the couples get into their cars and drive off.

I lagged behind till Marie slid into her car—she did sit for a long instant before she drove off.

I saw her once more—that very afternoon, late. I was leaning over the little wooden bridge that then crossed from what we called the Girl's Hole to Gull Pond and looked up to see Marie coming down the road to the beach. Gull Pond, a runoff from the bay, is a mere stone's throw from Gill's place. I wondered if she had had to go back, see or pass it with that perverse insistence in clinging with certain consolation to the most melancholy of memories She halted when she saw me, but for only an instant, and then came straight to me, smiling, though nothing could disguise the red eyes—perhaps she was walking in the wind to give reason to their redness or to allow them to pale to normal. With her hair loose now, she looked sadly liberated.

"Walk with me—please," she said.

That *please* pierced like an arrow.

Marie. I wanted to reach out and draw her to me. I wanted to break, confess all my years of distant feeling—love, adoration even. I wanted to spill—console her, rescue her from that heaviness, in an instant eradicate the irremediable past. I was seething with sympathy. But I could not speak. What could I say which would not hurt her more?

We walked. I watched her beautiful head, that perfect profile, raised to the wind. We walked the sand. She said nothing—as if there was no need to go beyond that simple invitation, which implied an unspoken bond between us—and let the wind speak of things swept away forever.

Even when we halted, she said nothing. Perhaps she feared a single word would release an uncontrollable torrent. Back at the bridge she took my hand, she kissed my cheek, she looked into me, then she turned back alone.

The next day she went back to France.

From the moment of the wedding, except at work, almost nobody saw Dick. It seemed a contrived disappearance. His earlier social life—the dining, yachting, fishing excursions, parties and outings—were clearly cut out of his life, an almost immediate shock to those he "ran around with," in his wife's terms: For at once Netta settled down as if to verify my grandmother's "the typical Polack"—for, immediately, out of whatever fidelity to his commitment to Netta or to his rejection of his past life (vicious, Netta must have thought) or intent "to keep the peace at home"—they were a bound pair in no way available even to their families, though during their first few months there was no way of Dick's avoiding the family drop-ins, though once they saw the house they were not much encouraged to return for it was as tiny as a storage shed, convenient "to save" though perhaps it was the only way to survive in a bad season, for every penny passed into Netta's hands and nothing was not "too expensive to waste a cent on." And as if to alienate his family further, when Dick did invite them—he must have felt it a conscience-ridden protocol—what they came upon was Netta in a straight bag dress sewn no doubt from flour sacks and with nothing underneath, Netta in bare feet, and Dick shirtless and shoeless. Presently she laid a dish out for each, took the pot of stew from the stove and set it in the center of the table, each to eat what he would out of it—and from no poverty but perversity, my grandmother claimed, to send us off irremediably, to hoard Dick for herself irremediably—and almost as if to prove her right, in no time Dick and Netta hied themselves off to an almost equally tiny house—"shack," my grandmother called it—a good hour's drive from town, just conveniently distant enough "to ditch us," she said.

And the distance disconnected Dick from his work contacts because—for whatever reasons, and in a bad economic moment for work, and with experience that required travel all over Long Island, a car and costs—Dick took (as he would go on for years taking) whatever job was available as near as possible to the house. "The woman's triumph," my grandmother claimed. And some years after, seeing how much Dick had changed, she would say, "And who but that woman would want him now?" And nobody could "steal Dick away" for a drive or visit or drink because Netta's law was no money wasted so "no beer and no booze in this house"; and whenever she could, Netta went to work like a man with him or lent a hand—clamming and crabbing and scalloping, sometimes housepainting, sometimes even helping to load or unload a truck or a freight car and in season doing lawns and gardening. Finally, with some years of stability, clearing the acres they had managed to buy with that little house stuck on one end, they went into the flower business, growing fields of exquisite mums of every variety, an ocean of colors where in season you could see Netta or Dick's head rise from deep in the mums, where from sunrise to sunset they worked from planting time through weeding and watering and cutting and packing mums to be shipped on the early morning train for sale at the New York market. So anyone seeing Dick looked around for the inevitable Netta.

Nobody, of course, mentioned Marie. And why would anyone? For wasn't she Dick's secret?

But on my visits, it was the one casual if crucial question, "And Marie?"

"Oh, Marie! She came, as always—in July, I think. I spotted her in church, as beautiful as ever. And she always stops to see the girls."

"And still single then?"

"Oh, you know those professional women—though who could possibly have more opportunities!"

"Yes, who!" I said.

"And you're as bad as she is, Hal. When am I going to have some great-grandchildren? It's a shame to waste somebody with your looks."

"But they might look like my wife!"

"You!"

But it was Dick I really wanted to ask about Marie. He had always been my favorite uncle and I never went to the Island without seeing him, and always I hoped he would reveal his life with Marie—for surely he had had one, that day at Gill's must have climaxed a long and secret relationship. He was always glad to see me, but my visits evoked a sadness in him, for sooner or later a moment would come when I would discover him staring at me with a kind of abstract fascination, with wonder. He admired my discipline and education and submergence in my world. And one afternoon he did say, "I never found the thing I had to do. I envy you that. I went from one thing to the other. I floated." "But you could have done anything!" I said. He gazed into the grass. "There was . . . were . . . those who offered me every opportunity, everything," he said, "but I had enough presence to know the impetus had to come from me, be born in me, to do whatever I had to do, or I'd become a burden to someone else and, worse, be responsible for that involvement in my life. I couldn't betray a faith in me which had no honest basis. I couldn't live a life that wasn't my own." I felt that desperation in him that sometimes only a deathly stillness reveals. We both went silent. A sadness descended over us; it bound us. I never loved him more. I wanted to take him into myself, make him me, so I could say, You see, you did do it. I might have said something to console him, but Netta called and crossed the lawn to us. Netta was a talker, filled with every detail, the greatest of observers and, despite all my grandmother's and the family's comments about "the Polack," she and I had always hit it off like cronies—if she seemed to ward off visitors, she never wearied of some few of her own choosing; and as I was one she fired questions at me, taking everything in; and she was as verbal on paper and kept me informed of everything happening in their immediate world in letters which she wrote all the years as if, liking me and my mother particularly, she had decided she would possess us as she did Dick.

But Dick would not be possessed, I was convinced. Had Dick—unconsciously—chosen not to choose a direction, moving toward some as yet undefined end subconsciously pursued? That choosing not to may have been a strange kind of salvation—because something in him had "chosen," pursued sacrifice. Had that begun the day he had rejected Marie or the day he had chosen Netta, perhaps the deliberated beginning of a path, not knowing then where it would lead? Down. His way was down. Did he know that? Could he have known that? If not, would he have pursued it?

Year after year, as I visited, his situation grew worse. The flower business finally failed and the failure demanded a new "dream" merely for survival; however small that dream, it was no less the daily dream, and necessary: How little could they live on in that house of minimal costs, how little wear, how little eat? Netta was always saving, never telling even Dick, I suspect, what they had. Even if they were to buy on credit, "charge it," they couldn't, they had no credit, they had always paid "cash and carry" for what few of their meager possessions they had actually bought new—and there was no one to buy for because the first child had been stillborn and buried back in the town cemetery, which Netta visited faithfully to pay homage to that gone possibility, and then Netta had had two miscarriages. Perhaps because there was no visible future, no future of their own flesh, no child to embody his own possibilities, as the years passed the dark wavy hair falling in two wings over his forehead grayed and his rich deep blue eyes seemed colder and indifferent and stared with a strange anonymity—farther, it seemed, not here. And he took a long chance—and with what recommendations?—and put in for janitor at the local high school and landed the job, to his disbelief and Netta's joy. It seemed almost a miracle to him after a lifetime of never a steady job at something he could take joy in.

So for some years—stability. He could not believe the benefits, the relief for Netta, not to have to touch savings, not to pay cash.

Security.

He could breathe now.

Now he lived three to twelve as custodian. He made it his place, the basement corner. He lived down there with something like relief, a period of rest, though he was industrious. He liked cleaning. The principal and teachers grew fond of him. Now and then talking to students, he marveled at how advanced this one or that was. And there he could ponder. I imagined him sitting sometimes in darkness, alone, the hermit, with those eyes turned inward on an invisible terrain, which he must be seeing, wondering where the next rise or turn would lead him. And I wondered where because more and more whenever I saw him these last years, he was abstracted, though physically there with me, yes, and responding to me and *Mother*, as he had come to call Netta after the loss of "the children." But there was an air of tranquil, even resigned, waiting in him. His presence was a strange comfort, particularly as his voice, the singer's strong baritone—perhaps from his being so much alone, with Netta doing most of the talking, and from working so many jobs by himself, or perhaps because he grew more evidently meditative as if talking to himself—softened, diminished so that it caused you to listen, very unlike the bold voice that had demanded no attention.

Yes, he could breathe now.

But not for long.

I lamented that my grandmother, who had taken an almost vindictive pleasure in pointing out Dick's increasing isolation and descent, had died before he became the custodian, though she would surely have seen him no longer as "self-employed" but as an "inferior" laborer, what, until her three sons, nobody in her family had been: Her people, she had pointed out, did the hiring for her family brick works. What neither she nor my aunts and Jared had ever asked was the why of Dick's degeneration. To them, I thought, Marie must never have existed. And Dick—with a cavalierly sense of honor?—remained secret and silent about Marie. To judge by his silence, she might never have existed for him either; but I had learned over the years that it is sometimes the thing one is absolutely silent about, the never mentioned mother or father or brother or lover, that holds the revelation.

And Marie—she continued coming to the Island: from what necessity? Beautiful and deceptively young, she came always in summer, if always briefly. My joy—rare—was to coincide with one of her visits to The Hall. Whenever she ran into me, she invited me to that sitter so sacred to my memory. And I was impressed with the way sometimes I caught her almost lost in staring at me. And after we had taken each other through some talk of plays, books, the Island, her cities, and my classes and research, I would give her a rundown of what had happened to the family since her last visit, in the most casual way dropping suggestions of what I felt she had come back for, bits of Dick's life, the only way in which I felt I could serve her, because there was nothing I wanted more than that, to be whatever part of Marie's life I could. She nodded but said nothing, though I knew she must be hoarding those inklings of his life, for, I asked myself, wasn't that really why she had come, why she would keep coming, for what little was left for her in town but memory to verify and nourish? And always when I left—she could not have been unaware all those years of my love for her—in her European fashion she kissed me on both cheeks and thanked me: for what? the visit? that little view into Dick's life?

It was my mother who in one of my weekly calls told me Dick had "come down with" cancer and had had a lung removed against his wishes, she said, but at Netta's insistence, despite the doctor's doubts that he would live that much longer; but of all the family the optimistic Netta most insistently lived with hope—and Dick was now, my mother said, "very low." The discovery must have been sudden. I should have suspected something because Netta's letters had fallen off though in a fairly short time.

What possessed me to call Dick one night, I don't know—I never had. Later I told myself it was an inexplicable communication from Marie, though at the time I'd had Netta and Marie on my mind since the talk with my mother. "Hal!" Netta cried. How relieved she must have been to hear a voice she loved interrupt her heavy and unceasing and agonizing tasks. Her joy was like a great cry of faith, which had brought unexpected support from a remote corner. And it had. She would never forget: "Dick kept saying 'Hal called. Imagine that. Hal called.' It made him so happy, Hal." But that night I couldn't tell he was happy. "Let me talk to Dick," I said. And there was so long an interval before he reached the phone that I thought something had happened. Then he whispered, "Hello, Hal." I could hear the strain—heavy, close, harsh breathing. How it wrenched him to speak! "Tell me about yourself," he said, so I talked all I could, with him whispering "Yes," "Fine," "Good." I felt I had to make some final offering to him before I hung up. I said, "Dick, we've bought Gram's house to keep it in the family, and town's one of the few places that's still pretty much as it was from the waterfront to The Hall, which Marie Bascomb still comes home to open up once a year." I heard his heavy breath and his noncommittal "Is that so?" but there was no word more from him, and after a silence Netta took the phone and said, "Dick's a little tired, Hal," and she talked for some time, repetitively, for what else could she do? I was relieved that her voice, heavy too now, did not break.

Dick died a few weeks later.

There is a crawl space under one side of the sloping roof over Dick's old bedroom in my grandmother's house. The following summer while renovating, my mother and I went through what had been accumulated in trunks and boxes or shoved into attic areas. In the crawl space—standing straight up so close against the bedroom wall I might have missed it—I came upon a large frame. "Why, it's Marie!" my mother said. "I *know* that portrait. Whoever would stick it there?" "Dick," I said. "Dick! But you don't suppose Marie and Dick—" I laughed. "Anything's possible." But I didn't share my secret except to say, "He probably didn't want Netta to see it." "She would've had a *fit*!" It was a familiar two-thirds profile of Marie, a black and white photograph—achingly beautiful to me and familiar because my aunts had once had a copy they had torn from the cover of *Cosmopolitan* magazine. She turned it over. "Look here! Why, it's for you, Hal!" On the brown paper backing was printed FOR HAL. Me! What had Dick seen? "But why—" My mother looked mystified. "But why *me*, you mean? Why not? I'm the youngest in the family." Had he feared Netta might destroy this one vestige of Marie? But I was quivering with the surprise—and joy—of it. I wanted to think he was surrendering Marie to me. Was he? Or insisting his and Marie's story on me? Whatever, Dick was giving me a sign. It bound me to him. He'd known my quiet tenacious curiosity. He must have known I would probe and ponder. He must have bet on that. Why? That someone would know and understand? No, it wasn't in Dick's nature to seek self-recognition or self-adulation, striving—if he had been—toward increased alienation and asceticism; but he was, as romantic stories say, "speaking from beyond the grave."

At the news of Dick's death, I immediately thought of Marie. Would she know? How? Was it only in summer that she caught up on the year's events or was there someone in town, her messenger, who wrote her a rundown?

In the long run was that what *I* was?

I took it into my own hands. She must know. It was imperative. And I wanted her to know. I too much wanted her to know. And I wanted to be the instrument of her knowing. That impulse was—as I see it now—an intentional, and natural, perversity. Sometimes, because I loved her I wanted her to suffer, or go on suffering. Would it be Dick's suffering? Or a parallel to his having made her suffer—so much so that as proof to him she had remained single all the years? Or a parallel to my own romantic suffering?

Was I, then, what bound them during the long separation, which they endured like chaste distant lovers who, no matter what the situation, are really imaginatively united? I wrote:

Since our "days in Rome" together years ago, much has happened on the Island. Our terrain, physical and emotional, has been slowly depleting and transformed. Town, always the same, nonetheless has its vacancies. Only shadows fill them, my grandparents', my parents', Paul's, Jared's—about them you know—and now Dick's—

I did not go into detail and tell her of Dick's last weeks and how he had suffered, as Netta had told me, but borne his suffering with the steadfastness of a saint.

Briefly I went on to tell her about my life—my university career—and of my good fortune in receiving a two-year appointment as lecturer at Oxford University with rooms at Pembroke College. I would be leaving for England soon, in early September.

I heard nothing from Marie, though I had no right to anything particularly personal. I did feel Marie might, since she was so correct, send a courtesy reply, and I dreamed of seeing a letter written in her hand.

At Pembroke, *Pemmie*, I had rooms on the ground floor of the Alms House, under the rooms of one of the dons, and lived spoiled by my scout, George.

It was almost two years—on a rarely beautiful day of neither rain nor fog, the emerald green of the quad and the blue of the sky stark—that Pontsford the porter sent George to me.

"You have a visitor, sir, in the porter's lodge."

"A visitor?"

"Yes, sir. Should I show her in, sir?"

"Her?"

"A lady, sir. I might add a most beautiful lady."

"Beautiful!"

"Like a picture, sir."

"I'll go and fetch her, George." George smiled, catching my use of the word he usually used for such occasions. "Will you bring us tea, please."

George, I'm sure, would rather I had not assumed his duty, but I was curious.

I had absolutely no thought of Marie as I crossed the quad, and when I looked up I felt an instant's joy and dread. Marie was standing smiling at me just outside the porter's lodge with Pontsford in his most gracious manner beside her.

Suddenly—for a curious instant—I was back on the Island, transported to sand, sun, church, all the old faces—

"Marie!" It was a cry of joy and a choke.

"Hello, Hal." She kissed me on both cheeks.

"I can't believe this," I said. "Are you sure we're not somewhere else?"

"If only we were."

I led her along the quad. "I've never seen such green," she said. "Oh," I said, "it's an Oxford pride, this centuries-old rolled grass." We descended the steps past the ablutions and turned at the wall to the Master's house and garden and took the steps down to my quarters in the Alms House. I told George tea. He nodded and left us alone.

"But what on earth are you doing in Oxford?" I said.

"Isn't it time I answered your letter? The truth is: I was visiting friends in London, and thought Oxford's too close to miss this opportunity to put myself straight with you. I don't often get letters from home. It was like being . . . Sometimes I feel the sea has hands that hold me and won't ever let me go . . . and . . . I don't want them to."

"I know. I used to wish I could swallow the sea and carry it inside me."

"*That*, yes!" She looked as if she had just glimpsed paradise, radiant.

Of course, she asked abut Hazel and Alice. I gave her a somewhat detailed rundown on everybody she knew. I was waiting for her to catch sight of her photo.

George interrupted and set out the tea things.

"May I do the honors?" she said.

I watched her pour, all grace. The light from the high spire-like windows fell over us and the silver glittered in her hands. In quick instants of repose, her head and her gesture seemed frozen for the camera, pensive, abstracted. Her hair, sleekly drawn back, emphasized her fine cheekbones and her deep green eyes and her complexion unblemished and her full unwithered lips. Who could have guessed she was Dick's age, and wearing, who had a generation on me. Looking at her, I couldn't help thinking She's mine, now Marie's mine, it could always have been like this—

"Nobody makes tea like the English," she said.

"So the English say."

At just that moment when she laughed she saw her photo over my desk. Only her interrupted gaze over her suspended cup spoke. The photograph gave me the opportunity to mention Dick, for how else could I do it without revealing what little I knew?

"I found it in the attic space by Dick's room."

"Oh?"

"He left it to me. *For Hal* he'd written on it. I carry it with me whenever I'm gone for long periods."

She seemed to ponder that.

"You were always special in his eyes. Dick was very loyal to what he loved."

"You knew that?"

She smiled. "I intuited that."

"And you trust to intuition?"

"Don't you?"

"Once I did. But not any longer. Facts have a way of intimidating intuition, perhaps even shriveling it, so that you don't trust it so readily."

"I hate to think that. It would cut off what most of us feel binds us."

"And not memory? I think that has a stronger case."

"You can't live on it."

"Many people do."

"If they do, it's because they bank on some possibility for the future alive in it."

"You really think that?"

"I know it."

My conviction, staring at her as I was, may have perturbed her.

"Sometimes," she murmured, "the future was yesterday."

I understood too much to say she was making riddles.

"Then you can't live with it."

"Sometimes memory alone has to be enough."

"No, *not* enough." She was clearly startled by my emphatic denial. "There has to be tomorrow; otherwise there's no fulfillment."

"Fulfillment is a dream which fails."

"Then you must make something of your failure. Maybe that's what failure's all about."

"You mean sacrifice yourself to failure—?"

"Yes." I was thinking: because the extent of sacrifice reveals the depth of what has been sacrificed. "If you give some meaning to the sacrifice . . ."

"Some meaning to the sacrifice . . .?"

Somehow that repetition—and a forlorn meditative stillness in her—stirred me. Her silence could always evoke thought in me. My words must have been as sharp as arrows, and the reverberation quivered not only in her but in me. Somehow *that*—sacrifice. Dick had sacrificed himself? He had sacrificed himself as the very measure of his love? He had refused her? He was not up to her, and he could not live on her money?

"But some would have sacrificed everything with no thought of meaning."

So had she been willing to give all to live that life with Dick? and he would not allow the sacrifice? The truth of that lanced me—that he loved her too much to take her down a destructive path, though she would have gone unreservedly. Rather, Dick chose the *other*, and sacrificed himself to that, and purely—by renouncing Marie, and purely. Since he would not reduce Marie to that life, he reduced himself both as a self-castigation and as demonstrable proof, yes, of the worth of his love: He submitted himself to Netta, to the purity of his sacrifice and the fulfillment of his duty, of whatever that love consisted. He let Netta reduce him as he might have reduced Marie. So that was why he left town shortly after the marriage, to get away from Marie's ambience—or else?

And Marie . . . There is a way even the tarnished keep themselves virginal. Marie—in turn—had chosen a similar path, the purity of her own sacrifice to a love that had been denied her. Or had saved her.

Saved her?

For *me*! I was thinking. I wanted to believe that even then Dick knew. Dick was handing her on to a love he had perceived was growing, maturing during all those years. Had Dick been watching *me*?

Suddenly the bells striking thundered and reverberated, vibrating the very air. Time was going, the sun, and the long shadows were cutting the daylight from the upper windows. She tilted her face up toward the sound.

"The bells of Christ Church—across the street."

"How grand—to live under that. The sound washes everything away"

"Not everything—and not for long. Some things withstand anything."

"I'm sure. But what?"

Netta crossed my mind—she stood there clearly. Netta: what she had. She had known all the years what she had. Even if she had known of Dick's love for Marie, hers was the triumph. She had had Dick. He was hers. In whatever way he might not have been hers, she must not have cared. There beside her he was real, her concern and her charge. And she had loved him completely, possessively, with certainty. What she could not touch did not seem to have concerned her. If it had, outerly she had never let it show.

But some essence, whatever Marie had shared with Dick—some essence beyond sex, beyond love—had Netta yearned for that too? Had she sometimes felt that the deepest silt had not been penetrated and stirred to ecstasy? It struck me then—so close to the source of Dick's dilemma, so close to Marie and her own, and mine—that Dick had not loved anybody or anything, that there was something in Dick—the deepest something, but particularly pronounced in him—which runs through star and stone and green, and that Marie had experienced that in Dick and it had touched her deeply, too deeply—as it must not, *must* not—because its truth too much hurts. That experience damages the immediate, this *now*. That essence is a terrible and beautiful extremity rare between two people, who go beyond self to more than self, or all. One lived with it, one had to, because the experience could never be undone and nothing might ever again evoke it, an extremity not love and which, because it is beyond love, no man can violate.

Forlorn, I thought that terrible—or wonderful?—thought.

And in answer to her "But what?" I said, "Love. Or I could call it fidelity to the desire one has had all his life."

"Desire?"

"Dream—the same thing. Marriage to your dream. And you have never needed that . . . marriage?"

"In my heart . . . I've always been married."

Time threatened. I could have cursed time, cursed all the years.

"But not married." Again I thought *Netta*. "There are the long days, the sometimes interminable hours . . . You're never lonely at Seine-et-Oise?"

"Loneliness can be very exaggerated. That too becomes absorbed as a normal part of daily life. The world is always there." She smiled. "And we can always go back over bits of it." And rose. It was as if she had succeeded in divesting herself of her very sensuality.

"Marie—" I caught her elbows. "Listen—"

Her eyes met mine, her smile vanished, I felt apprehension in her slight tremor.

"All my life, since childhood even, I've loved—"

Abruptly her hand rose and her fingers pressed my lips silent.

"Yes," she said and for the briefest second her eyes closed and her lips trembled; then withdrew her hand, and so incredibly softly said, "Yes, Hal."

How could I think she had not known of my love all the years, as women do?

"But I *have*—"

"It won't—"

"Won't?"

"—won't do."

Then she said, "Come. Walk me to the gate. I'd like to walk from there to the station alone."

We ascended the sets of steps, passed the ablutions, the quad, and Pontsford reading in his window in the porter's lodge. One side of the great door was open. She turned to me, filled I could see to breaking, and for an instant I shifted my eyes to St. Aldate's cemetery behind her. "I can't tell you what it's been, this meeting," she said, "but you know." And she took my head in her hands and looked at me long and this time kissed me on the mouth long too and did not loosen my head but stood staring, her eyes much too still and threatened with emotion. And in that instant I knew whom she saw. I knew why she had come. I knew who I was now. And *she* knew who I was. I was tempted to think there was a kind of vengeance in her rejection of me, almost a perverse desire to make me suffer, to sacrifice me for his sacrifice of her. Something had ended—for her. Something was placed—for me. *It won't do.* But no. I was no longer Heathcliff. In an act of mercy—mercy?—had she refused me? I knew I would not see her again. She freed my face and regained an apparent ease and turned out the gate and followed the college wall to the street. She did not look back. I watched her turn up toward the Carfax and disappear.

At Christ Church the last of sun was moving up Tom Tower.

They were passing the beach ball on the sand. It went from Chet to Ron to Ben to Chet. The boys hadn't been home together in years. For an instant Ward had the illusion that his sons were kids again and that he would join the play. Then the boys retreated somewhere into those men's bodies, and Chet's wife Ellie and Ron's Sandra were here to prove the years gone. Only the grandchildren had copped out, all three ready to start their fall semester. Chet clearly resembled him at forty, a little slack—"comfortable" Ruth called it. Ben—he had Ruth's sensitivity—was a rod and, surprisingly, all muscle and sinews now—from his "ecological" life, no doubt. Ron? In looks he might have been "the plumber's son." The politician, all attractive image and as adaptable as a chameleon, he could fill in for any absent male in the TV soaps.

Ward resented his own body being entrenched in the beach chair. You had to watch the heart. Still, he'd gone at it hot and heavy this long weekend, for exercise had even rowed Ellie and Sandra a short way around the jut toward Plum Gut. Tomorrow they'd all be gone. You could see they were all tired, tried perhaps, and ready for their own nests. Tomorrow it would be Ruth and sea and sand and sky and gulls. Ruth grew nervous as the time approached. It didn't show, but he knew.

Happily, this last afternoon—late now—was summery, rare for Labor Day week, with only the slightest breeze, great for charbroiling. The smell of meat was mouth-watering. The Sound lay almost serene, lapping with soft ripples. The sun was lowering. Opposite, the Connecticut shore was still unusually clear.

He heard Ellie and Sandra break into laughter at something Ruth said as they carried the food out. All weekend Ruth had pumped the girls full of the boys' history. Recalling stimulated her. When would she have such a chance again? And Ellie and Sandra couldn't get enough; they wanted to know their men through and through.

A cry broke from Ron.

"Missed!" Chet said.

The ball shot past Ron, struck a boulder, veered sharply, landed some distance out on the water, and stilled, floating.

For an interval they were all still as a photo, staring at the ball. Then for no reason everybody laughed. Ben dashed down the sand, crossed the band of white stones and took a running dive in. His head came up not far from the ball. He gave it a blow and it rose high and Chet caught it and stood holding it.

Ellie said, "Steaks are on. Better put your order in." "I'll get the baked potatoes," Sandra said, but if anybody heard them, nobody responded—because there was a murmur from Ruth, "Oh, no," her hand rose, she took a step toward the beach and halted, her face apprehensive, and they too followed her gaze: because Ben had turned and headed out, his powerful strokes making a swift glide.

"The little bastard," Chet mutterred, but it carried.

"He *would*," Ron said.

"What?" Sandra turned a mystified face to Ron.

"Look at him go!" Ellie set the tray down.

"Ben," Ruth called, but not loud, "don't go out too far."

"He can't hear out there, can he?" Sandra said.

"Voices really carry over water," Ward said.

"Ruth." Ward reached for her hand.

"Please," she said to him.

He said. "But you know how he loves the water, and he's an ace swimmer."

But he knew it wasn't that.

"Come on," Chet said. "I'll turn the steaks, Ellie." He turned his back on the Sound and went up the steps to the deck.

Far out, Ben stopped swimming. His head, tiny from here, rode the surface, still as that ball. Then it went under—and stayed—and long: till Ward thought, *Why, Ben's doing it deliberately.* He stood, impatient, but stared too, motionless. No Ben. Where in hell was he!

Ruth murmured something, too low to hear. But her frantic eyes told.

"Well," Ron said, "he can't stay under forever. No telling where the devil'll come up."

"Ron!" Ward said—too sharp.

It was, for Ruth especially, an agony of waiting before Ben's head bobbed up as if from some secret depth. Ruth gasped, relieved, but only for an instant because Ben started swimming out again.

"Oh, no," she said.

"It's all right, Ruth," he said.

Undeterred, she stood vigilant.

"That's just like him," Chet said.

"Why, he's a marvelous swimmer! Look at him go. If I could swim like that, I'd never stop," Sandra said.

"Sandra!" Ron said.

"Well, for heaven's sake!" she said. "A man can't have a swim?"

"He may not stop, if I know anything," Chet said.

"All *right*, Chet!" Ward said.

"Well, he doesn't have to drive it home, Dad."

"Chet's right, Ward," Ruth said. "I guess I'm just getting to be a sensitive old woman. Ask your father—he'll tell you."

"Well, why shouldn't you be?" Sandra said.

Ruth smiled. "Come on, everybody. I guess Ben knows what he's doing. Everything's laid out. Chet's taking orders. I want mine well done, Chet."

Leave it to Ruth to save the moment.

But Ward didn't miss her last quick glance out.

At the grill, Chet, a drink in one hand, still managed efficiently. Always did. The oldest. Responsible. Ordered. By the book. A mania for precision. "Bloody, rare, medium well, well—name it now or forever hold your peace," Chet said. You'd hate to be submitted to his impatience with carelessness. It showed in his two boys. Small wonder Bick and Ralph went off to the U early. Hard to believe a son looked so like you—and more and more with time—but so different inside. What went on in Chet? Somehow it was his control you admired—his workers must—or his pride in near perfection, with minimum waste. Maybe that was contagious. But who'd want the continual pressure? Maybe at home he took it out on Ellie. Growing up, he'd tried to run the boys. The son father. Natural in the oldest. Run Ron. But not run Dean. Nobody ran Dean.

What *had* run Dean?

He saw Dean now in that body stroking vigorously in toward shore. Ben. What had happened to Ben? Had Ben wanted to *be* Dean?

You'd had so little time for any of them, but it was always Dean you took, Dean always ready and waiting, and you not aware until he'd gone that he was the chosen—and Dean the last one surely even to *think* chosen, though the older boys might have thought that at the time and been jealous, surely Ben, because youngest, who'd depended on Dean, Dean his bible. You should have realized their resentment—you and Dean fishing, hunting deer upstate, attending the powwows in the Hamptons: the boy so spontaneous with a lust to experience and go into, as if there were something in him—his eyes would dart restless and then stare long—that couldn't stop moving. He was raw life, pure, but nothing could live pure and raw for long—it broke free or life tamed it.

Where he and the boys would halt, Dean would lunge. Dean had no fear.

Chet forked the meat. "Bring your plates."

Ellie kissed Chet on the forehead. "I'm absolutely starved."

"Food's on the table. Help yourself, everybody." Ruth turned lively, assured, now that Ben was approaching shore. For a long time after Dean, she couldn't bear to look out at the Sound; she was afraid when wind and storm riled the waves into a chaos and except in calm weather refused to cross from Orient Point to New London because the ferry had to go through the Gut—

"Well, don't just sit there, Ward. Self-service." Ruth kept him moving—good for the old ticker.

But Sandra intervened. "Let *me*." She filled a plate. "Your dad's, Chet—medium well, remember." Quick, with charm, she knew how to handle. The perfect politician's wife. She bolstered Ron. He'd end up in Congress, the senator from California, and Sandra a major asset—or one of them—because Ron had a scent for mass opinion—on higher education, illegal immigrants, the death penalty, abortion—and right or wrong he bet on that scent. "The illegals are costing the state a fortune, taking jobs, eating up benefits, increasing police and legal fees." Ron couldn't stay off it, but Sandra'd face him on the issues. "You simply can't reduce the problem to money alone, Ron. What on earth do we represent if we don't champion the underdog. We can't lose our humanity. It's what this country *means*. You have to look at what the illegals contribute." "And what do they?" "Worlds of vital culture. Besides, they compete, the American worker needs the jolt, maybe the illegals will help restore our work ethic." "At the expense of the state's going broke?" "Apparently New York City's well on the way to it too," Ruth said. Not for nothing Ron's form and his Reagan smile and the ever close Sandra. You don't have to act for us, Ron. Why did he? Was he born acting, couldn't help it?, the three-letter man on the field, or had something made Ron choose the comfortable path? But Ward had to hand it to Sandra—she had a mind of her own, she could set Ron straight. Of course you loved Ron, loved all the boys, each one differently, maybe for their weaknesses—or your own. You can't cure weakness. Sandra must know. She's Ron's strength. Ron's what she needed to realize her own. Something in us spots the weakness our own weakness needs. And Ben? What had *he* needed?

Ben was close to shore now.

"Spend a day in the computer business, Sandra, and you wouldn't so easily dismiss the American worker." Chet. You could believe him too: drive, production, sales. He knew how to meet change.

"I'll take you up on that, Chet." Sandra laughed.

"Oh, Sandra, you don't know what you're in for," Ellie said.

"I'd have burned your steak for that, hon," Chet said.

Ellie laughed. In her forties, she still laughed and moved seductively. She'd been the family surprise. *Cold* they'd always thought Chet. Well, you were closed out of that part.

Ben had come up on the sand and was sitting resting, his arms around his drawn-up knees, and gazing out. What was he seeing?

"Ben, come on in. Ben!" Ruth called.

"He'll come when he gets ready to. You know Ben," Ron said.

"That's for sure," Chet said.

"Has he always been that independent?" Sandra said.

"They all are, if I'm any judge," Ellie said.

"And are you?" Chet said.

"Ha! Enough of that now," she said. "Drink, Ward?"

"Scotch, straight. Doctor Spurling said my heart can take Scotch but nothing else."

Ben stood, halted a moment, then turned and sprinted over the sand and up the steps to the deck.

"It's great under—a rich year for seaweed. You should see it where the ledge dips, it's dense and long, a jungle down there."

"Seaweed gives me the willies," Sandra said.

"And me," Ruth said.

"Steak, Ben?" Ellie said

"Thanks, Ellie. I don't eat meat."

"Since when?" Ron asked.

"Since." Ben looked across at Chet.

Chet met his stare. "Since?"

"Yes," Ben said.

"Well, there are salads galore to choose from, and vegetables, Ben." Now that Ben was back safe, something—Ruth's delayed irritation?—returned.

"Ruth," Ward said, "while you're at it, would you serve me a little more potato salad? It's great."

She caught his look and came for his plate.

"Well, Ben didn't have to do that," she said.

Ben heard. "But I *did*."

"Oh, Ben," she murmured.

Ward said, "Now, mother—" *Mother.* He hadn't called Ruth that in years! How spontaneously it had sprung from him, no doubt because all the boys were here for the first time since—

Since.

Now *why* had Ben loosed that dark cloud over the day.

Ben perched on a corner of the deck, his plate balanced on his knees. "The avocado salad's first-rate, Mom."

Sandra dragged her chair over and sat close. "Why no meat, Ben—a religious preference, or you just don't like it?"

"Sandra," Ron said.

"Am I being nosy, Ben?" she said.

"Yes, but why not?" He laughed. "Dead things repel me. All my work's dedicated to keeping things alive."

"Well, you obviously don't need it. You keep plenty healthy."

"It's the work. I'm outdoors all I can be, if never enough to suit me."

"He'd live in the woods if he could, and never come out," Chet said.

"Why bother? There's everything you need there."

"Except people," Ron said.

"People! I've had enough of them for one lifetime."

"Why, Ben!" Ruth said.

"Well, it's true. Bad enough that people mess up their own lives, but you should see what they're doing to the rain forests."

"Nobody grieves so much as Ben about the loss of a rain forest," Ward said.

"They grow back, don't they?" Ron said. "We're always planting trees."

"That's exactly what they don't do. We can plant trees, but we can't make forests. It takes millions of years of complex mutual dependence for a forest to develop. The biggest blight is people. They can't let nature alone. In their zeal for jobs and money, they're too blind to see that what we're trying to preserve will one day save them."

"What you mean is you want to be alone," Chet said, "because you don't like people."

"Chet!' Ellie said.

"Well, it's true," Chet bit.

"Is it so hard to imagine somebody loving plants and butterflies and birds more than people?"

"Yes."

"Well, I have my reasons. And forests are beautiful. If you didn't have beauty in your life, all this would be terrible."

"How come you don't retreat for good to your rustic paradise in the rain forest of Costa Rica, then?" Chet said.

"Don't think I wouldn't like to. Frankly, economics."

"Well, what's *wrong* with people?" Sandra said. "They've done something to you? I mean, it's not natural, is it?"

"Natural for me. Or I've made it so." He smiled, but looked off, far.

"But why have you?"

"My work demands solitude."

"But not your whole life?"

"Why not? It's my life. And is there anything wrong with trying to save something?"

"Why, Ben!" Ruth said.

"For heaven's sake, Sandra," Ron said.

"Ron, what gives here? We're just having a conversation. After all, when have I had a chance to get to know Ben?"

"Nobody gets to know Ben," Ron said.

"Dean did."

Dean.

"Oh, for Chris' sake, Ben!" Chet said.

"Chet!" Ellie said.

"Oh, boys, eat. Your steaks will be *cold*." Ruth's voice went thick.

Dean.

He was standing in the midst of them now, a presence.

Why had Ben called Dean up? Now he wouldn't go away. Ben wouldn't let him die. The truth is the shadow of Dean had come in Thursday night with Ben. "I'll take Dean's room," he'd said.

Dean. You could imagine how the fishermen had found him, washed in after four days sucked under and battered . . . He'd had to go to the city to identify him. *My son, yes.* But that bloated water-soaked flesh had not been Dean—Dean's flesh but not Dean. What had been Dean had vanished, escaped from that distorted flesh. Sometimes Ward thought the four boys were one person and none could be complete without the others. Dean had been the fire in them, and the fire had gone out.

Why didn't Ron ever talk of Ben? Was the politico ashamed of a brother for going off the deep end when Dean had drowned, for going strange and staying single and hooking on to nobody? Maybe Chet never talked of Ben either. If Sandra didn't know, what did Ellie? Had Ben become the outcast only because he couldn't get over Dean?

"What's Dean got to do with this?" Chet said.

"Everything," Ben said.

Yes, Dean had had everything to do with Ben's grief. Breakdown? Call it that, though Ben wouldn't have. How can I live without Dean? Ben had said. And said: I wish I were *with* Dean wherever he is, if you want to know. And it was futile for Ruth and him to insist that Ben continue his treatment because, after a small fortune spent on the psychiatrist, Ben confessed that therapy did, and *would* do, no good: He was grieving, he clung to his grief, he wanted his grief, some do and for long periods. Ben knew he was a victim of his own sensitivity. He had a capacity for too much love, an obsession with a one-to-one relationship; he didn't *want* to undo that love.

"Well, it's certainly obvious somebody here needs to talk," Sandra said

"There's a time for talk, Sandra," Ron said. "Besides, there's talk and talk."

"What's talk got to do with it?" Chet said.

"What's talk ever got to do with anything—but everything," Ben said.

"*Ben—*" But Ruth turned to *him*: "Ward?" But he was too caught now by Ben. Ben was not now the isolate. He was standing at the rail. Apart, against the sea beyond, he looked thinner and taller than he was.

"I don't understand," Sandra said.

And Ellie said, "You never told me the details, Chet."

"What've the details got to do with it?"

"Everything," Ben said.

"Damn it, Ben! The fact is Dean was drowned. He behaved like a fool," Chet said.

"That's no reason for *you* to." Ellie lay her hand on Chet's shoulder, but he shook free of it.

"What in the devil's that supposed to mean? You're losing me again," Sandra said.

"What he means, Sandra, is each to his own life," Ron said. "Let sleeping dogs lie."

"What dogs?" Sandra insisted, but it was Ben she faced.

"Dead ones," Ben was looking at Chet.

"Yes, dead," Chet said, "so let's have a drink to it."

"Two," Ron said.

"But I made lemon meringue pie, Chet. It was always your favorite," Ruth said.

"Not Chet's, Mom—Dean's," Ben said.

"It was? But how could I confuse . . ."

"Ben, tell me what Dean was like," Sandra said.

"Hasn't Ron?"

"What's to tell?" Ron said. "That was a long time ago. Besides, you didn't know him, Sandra."

"That's my point. We *should* know family. One of these days Millie will want to know what she came from."

"But Dean was drowned twenty years ago, and that's the end of it," Ron said.

"There's never an end to anything," Ben said.

You had to let go, Ben. You could agitate grief till you festered with the disease.

"Chet never did like to talk about it," Ellie said.

"Well, people should be able to talk about things after so many years," Sandra said. "Besides, God knows when we'll have a chance to talk family again."

"Sandra's right," Ruth said. "It should be a comfort. With time the moments you remember become the truest treasures you have."

Poor Ruth. Dean was ours, yes, but mostly hers, what she'd carried. Something always stayed with the mother, something—what—that wasn't severed with the cord.

"How'd it happen?" Sandra said.

Chet filled his glass. "Do we have to dredge that up again?"

"But we never *have*, Chet," Ellie said. "What's the harm?"

"We haven't either, have we, Ron?" Sandra said.

Ron shook his head.

"How'd he drown, Ben?" Sandra insisted.

But Ben said, "You tell her, Chet." After the drowning, Chet was the one who had been most in control and told it.

Ben crossed to the opposite side of the deck, stood looking out at the Sound, then turned to face them—as if he had stepped outside the scene.

Was he watching them all?

"Go on, Chet." Ben's voice vibrated.

What *is* this with Ben and Chet?

Chet said, "The four of us were swimming off Orient Point—by the Gut."

"Where you rowed us, Dad?" Sandra said. *Dad.* She made the word a comfort. Pity she and Ron and the children didn't live closer.

"Well, Plum Gut's a long way from the stretch we reached, Sandra, but when we drove out to the Point Saturday you saw the Orient light and the Plum Island lighthouse—the Gut's the strait between the two islands."

Chet said, "You'd have had to know Dean to understand how irrational he could be. All you had to say was *You can't* and Dean would go for it."

"I like him already." Sandra laughed.

"What Chet means is nobody swims the Gut," Ron said, "because there's always a powerful undertow, but when the tides meet, the water churns, you'd swear it was boiling. It makes the ferry from New London throb and vibrate so you'd think the hull was being shattered. No, nobody swims the Gut."

Chet told the drowning much as he had that day: "Dean had this sudden impulse to swim the Gut. He dived in and headed for Plum Island. We called and called, but he wouldn't turn back. The more we called the harder Dean plowed ahead. Ben kept shouting for Dean to come back. Dean headed right into the whitecaps. The sky was all gray, but it got dark and heavy fast. Who expected the sudden wind? And it started to rain. Then it came down hard. The rain whipped up the Gut so we had a hard time spotting Dean. He kept disappearing. Ben shouted and shouted. Then we couldn't see Dean's head. He'd gone under and never came up. Ben was screaming, he started in after Dean. It was all we both could do to hold him. We had to go call somebody, but Ben wouldn't leave. We were afraid he'd go in after Dean, so Ron stayed and I ran back to the first house, the Waddells', and called the Coast Guard."

"And?" Ellie said.

"They didn't find a trace of Dean. He was washed ashore miles up the Island. Ben lost his voice. He couldn't talk for days."

"Oh, Ben," Sandra said.

Weeks Ben was mute, and longing, longing for Dean, longing to die, yes, and poor Ruth half-mad with fear that Ben would do something to himself or that his voice wouldn't come back, and he, Ward, insisting, Give him time, time, hon, trying too to ease his own fears.

"Dean thought he was Lord Byron swimming the Hellespont," Chet said.

"So you said. But Dean never *mentioned* Lord Byron," Ben said. "Did he, Chet?"

What was Ben trying to do?

Chet was silent.

"Did he, Ron?"

"I don't know. It was all too quick. It's too far back to remember."

"Some moments are *never* too far back to remember, Ron. Dean said— Let me remind you what Dean said. He said, 'I guess I can't swim that cauldron.' "

"Something like that," Ron said.

Ben crossed the room and halted just behind Ward's chair, almost beside Chet. "And then what?"

You'd have thought some creature had stung Chet still.

"I don't think I want to hear this," Ruth said.

"Ben, damn it!"

Impervious, Ben waited.

Something—though every word Chet and Ron and Ben had spoken might have been the truth—something was missing.

Ward had never seen Chet struck helpless. He felt stricken for him. *Why?* He feared why. "Ben!" But Ben was not himself either: He was too bold for Ben; he had ventured out of his woods. As if he had learned stillness, as poised as any insect, he waited. When Chet did not speak, Ben said, "Yes. Dean said, 'I guess I can't swim that cauldron,' and he *wouldn't* have—" Ben dropped his voice so that surely only Ward and Chet heard him whisper, "if someone hadn't said *Byron would have*." Chet mouthed those words *Byron would have*. And Ben raised a clenched fist and raised his voice. "That made Dean tear free—he swung around and took a running leap into the Gut and swam for dear life . . ." Ben turned away, left them again, as he murmured, "And lost it . . ."

Ruth's eyes watered. She held her head still.

Don't—not to your mother. Ben.

"What is this?" Ellie's voice turned irritated. "Chet?"

"I don't get this," Sandra said.

You can't accuse—not your own brother, Ben. Chet wouldn't—and Ron wouldn't—

But Ward could not *un*think it.

He saw Chet's chest strain. "I don't have to listen to any more of this."

"You won't," Ben said.

Chet strode past him. "Anybody need a refill?"

"Later." Ellie followed after. "*I* need to start throwing our things together."

"Sandra?" Ron said.

"I'd better go up too."

Ron halted long enough beside Ben to murmur, "That was pernicious."

"Life's pernicious," Ben said.

"Then why make it worse?"

"You see why I prefer lichens."

But there was no triumph in Ben's voice, and none in his face. He turned away, stood at the railing, looking out to sea. Purged? Had he sought this last separation?

Would he let Dean go at last?

Within, all the lights went on. Shadows sprang up. Light made the night darker.

Ben had made Chet acknowledge his jealousy of Dean. Was that what he wanted? Because I couldn't help giving in to Dean—or myself? What'd I do to Chet? Neglected him. Threw responsibility on him. Never said *You're the oldest*, but always *Chet. What does Chet think?* as if the forethought were the boy's, the decisions his. Chet's every precise action he did to please me? Ron made his own way, adjusted to everything and everyone because he had to. Ben couldn't because I, yes, I took his companion from him, grounds, if I'd thought, not just for resentment, but hate—hate enough to devour Ben: because hate reveals how fierce love can be, and terrible—it binds you forever.

Chet would never forget this moment—*had* he ever forgotten that other?—if Ben's claim *were* true. Ward yearned to believe it was *not*: Whose was ever the real truth?

There you go again! Wanting to turn your eyes from what stared right into you.

"You had to do that, Ben?"

For a long moment only the waves sounded, soft on the shore.

"Yes. Wouldn't you have?" Ben said.

"Accuse my own—" He stifled his own breath.

"*I'm* your son too," Ben said.

Ward's heart rushed, his temples throbbed.

Ben. Oh, Ben.

How suddenly you were the father—and then not.

All the years had Ben been nurturing that moment?—not for Chet, but for *me*?

He was sure the boys would not come back again, at least not together, but it was not Ben . . . or Chet . . . who drove them away.

What have I done?

Condemned myself? For being weak, clumsy? Love stumbles.

And condemned, like Chet, to acknowledge what I've done?

In his silence to Ben he had confessed that.

Ben.

At the railing Ben was dark against the farther dark.

The last red was gone from the sky. The close shore was turning dark. After packing and changing, the others would come out and sit in the dark with them, as on the three nights before, and talk and watch the lights glimmer on the far Connecticut shore, or a freighter head toward the Atlantic, or the moon and stars, and, between words, listen to the indifferent wind and waves and leaves.

On the sand below, his beach chair was hardly visible now.

Ruth came out.

"They'll be down shortly." She rested a hand on his shoulder. He could not disguise his tremor.

"Ward?"

He knew her hand sensed all.

He said, "I'd better go down and rescue my chair before the tide carries it off."

"I'll go for it, Dad," Ben said.

He watched Ben dash down the steps and sprint over the sand.

And he waited.

LIB

She could hear voices—they were in the walls, the floors—but she could not hear their words. Sometimes she was sure they were voices lingering from a far time. Then Jarvis's laugh would crack, reminding. And she would hear the emptiness in the house, for they were all in the cellar, the entire family. All season they opened scallops down there, the six. Half the night their voices went on until they finished, exhausted. It was hard to get the kids to wash before they fell into bed—and almost before they were asleep, she was waking them, trying to get them off to school. Jarvis would keep them home—she had to battle as if she were their mother, and mostly lose, for they preferred to go off with their father, in dark, in boots, carrying their nets and buckets and burlap bags down to the rowboats at the crick to head out against the deepest gray sky. You could see them coming out of the dark, already in the rowboats as the greeny yellow dawn began to come over the bay.

And if she listened now, it was for the voice that would not come, a silence that made his presence resound more emphatically than their voices. He would be in the circle working with a studied face, the left side of his lower lip sucked under so that she would say, "You opening those scallops with your mouth or that knife," making them all laugh but Jarvis, who would grim his lips, whip his knife in sleek scoops, and gut the muscles from the shells faster. No, she did not miss the taut lips.

But there was fact: A year ago, and every year before, Kate would be opening with them, fast as any man, side by side with him. But Kate was dead.

She was Kate. Whatever of Kate she assumed, she bore, she continued. Wasn't she the older sister? Hadn't she brought up all the children? If Kate out of love, passion, for Jarvis had carried them (Kate had loved carrying his children, caressing him in his children, bearing him to the world), hadn't she raised them all the years in this house? She was their mother, if *not* their mother, for Kate had gone almost at once after each birth to housecleaning, meticulously, impeccably, but leaving shambles and wallowing in disorder at home. She had come to tend the first, Dennie, and she had stayed—they would never know why, it was no business of theirs, you went where you went toward fulfillment. Because Kate and Jarvis had expected it. Because she had known she would carry whatever it was she carried. Place, time, made no difference—fulfillment would be found, and somewhere. There were sensations, connections, which she knew and they did not—and there were no words. You moved and moved. So the motion went on. She stayed. Dennie, eighteen now, "her" first, Llewellyn the year after, three more years to Ruth and two to Travis and one to Dorothy—whom she had all but conceived and nursed. Hers, but not. And she theirs, but not.

So, beyond death, you stayed on. You waited for what would come, in whatever form.

She went down and put water on for their chocolate and coffee and set out milk, and went outside. How warm the Indian summer air! She halted to let her face and breasts and thighs feel its warm touch and then raised the cellar door. The fish odor assaulted, and a dank salt sea smell, and their voices. In day in the cellar there would be the interminable buzzing of flies which bred and madly on the odor alone, sudden new green gold life that gleamed under the electric bulb. It did no good, days, to air the cellar with the door open; the flies multiplied. She went down now. The closed-in odor of earth floor and dry beams assaulted too.

"About finished?"

She kept her distance. She was no interruption in their circle around the bushel bags. The plop-plops of scallops cut out and flicked exactingly into the buckets went on. Under the raw bulb, their faces, tanned as they were, looked white as the scallops. In the filled buckets the small bay scallops mounted like pupilless eyes. If the men were quiet now, surely it was because it was deep into morning and they were near dead.

Jarvis said, "We've hit bottom," nodding toward the burlaps. "Go on, the rest of you. I'll get these ready for the depot." There was a bite in his voice, so she dared not eye the boy but saw beside him a filled bucket and knew he was mastering speed to keep up with the others and open his just share. He kept his head down, insisted, it seemed, on making himself an island; and she felt a flush warm her, and went back up, warmed doubly outside, halting again to feel the friendly October breeze.

Dennie, a head taller than his father, all jackknife angles, bounded past her, hounded by Llewellyn hindered by heavy legs and enormous buttocks, which she helped along as he passed, laughing. "Stop, Lib!" He was shy with the boy there, and bounding into the kitchen he and Dennie slugged down their milk and were gone up to bed by the time Ruthie and Travis and Dot, three look-alikes, their towheads clean glows under the light, sat at the table a minute. Travis with his usual sulk said, "Do I have to—" "*Don't*," Ruthie mimicked Lib, "don't you start now, Travis. *Yes*, you have to go to school in the morning," and she and Dot burst into laughter and poked him. "Don't don't don't—" "Now stop that, girls, or he'll never sleep he'll be so mad. You *all* go to school this morning. You *report*." But she knew—between sickness, trickery, hookey, or Jarvis's bold intervention ("I need them at home"), they would work either for three hours before school or after a quick reporting in at school. She had kept order but she couldn't fight Jarvis's skirtings. Though she ran the house, it was his; she was subjected to that. "You kids *wash*," she said. "Bad enough scallops stinking up the whole house day and night, and you, Jarvis, I can't fight flies and stink and keep changing the beds every morning because you're all too tired to wash. I'm tired too." He drank his coffee, standing—and sullen, she saw. She had to call the boy in. Polite, he'd stand in the entry half the night, not to intrude, and each night he seemed to wait until Jarvis went to bed. Jarvis had taken to leaving at once, to make room for him, it would seem, as if the kitchen were too small, an illusion because the boy (*boy* she thought him, but he must be near thirty) was tall and wide and his beard gave solidity to him. Between her and Jarvis, when alone, the talk had become ritual: "How's he doing?" "Picking up." Jarvis meant, if begrudgingly, he was a worker. "You don't know he's there," he added. "*You* wouldn't know you were there in his condition." When he glanced up, she knew she'd been too quick. "He'll be a help to you," she added. "He's outside. He likes the night." Jarvis went up to his room in his dirty clothes, cankering her. By the time she'd poured the coffee for Random, she'd heard the knock and turned to see him through the backdoor pane.

She had been down on her knees in the yard cutting back the roses, September sun down the maple, when the shadow fell over her in bright day. Her breath caught. She looked up to a dark form, a dark head, shag, and a beard, wide shoulders—a man and young—but he was not close but for his shadow. And if she waited for speech, her eyes measured and gauged in the interval—the five children had trained her to that. He was still too long and vigilant—wary, evidently, the eyes unblinking and watchful, brown, very soft. Yes, wary. She knew a hurt creature—dog, rabbit, or man; what the others did not know was what she could become. And though she rose to him, even saying, "Well?," she realized—from his body, the poised head, the hands that rose and in quick rhythm became speaking, as if she knew signs—he could not speak.

"You can't talk."

He smiled, for his hands were speaking, then laughed maybe at how obvious it was.

"You're hungry?"

Not hunger, but work, he made clear.

"I've a houseful of men and girls."

She tremored at the dark doubt—had she cast a blight?—as

his lids fell, as if puzzled by lies he could not know, so her voice leaped, "My sister's, not mine," as if that made a difference. She had said it before she could wonder what released her. "She died last year. Kate loved having children but not caring for them. She did housework, hired herself out. Isn't that strange with a house and man and one baby after the other till she had five? She'd clean and clean but never touch her own, or maybe wanted to escape—oh, she loved them, and him, mostly him I think, if you want to know," and halted. His presence and the talk made her know again, amid all the luxury of a houseful, she had been lonely for Kate, who had been impervious to *her* life, Libby's. What that boy had let in like a jag of lightning heightened the long loneliness among the loved and her pity for him, for what a pole apart he was. And she saw too in his soft brown eyes a pity she did not want but which flattered. And she clammed up.

To gather herself to—for allowing his presence to break the shell of routine and spill her into air and green and against the thorns of roses—she was thankful for the solidity of a rake, which she carried to the cellar door area where, when they carted their shells, buckets, equipment, Jarvis and the others had scattered bits of shells with the dank too human smell of fish rotting, which bred those sudden gold-green flies.

Rebuffed, the boy was moving off. She felt the blight of his going.

"It's scallop season. They come home after dark, late, and open most of the night in the cellar. They might use a hand. He doesn't like to. It's good money. I could talk to Jarvis."

Now his eye gauged.

When he nodded, she actually laughed.

"You don't need anything, there're spare boots, the work's easy once you get the hang with the knife, and fast. You could sleep in the cellar, or I could pack you into the back entry on a cot. In this town there's a rush to get to the scallops first. They strip the scallop beds empty. To be truthful, it's mean—cutthroat." And to let subside the rush, desired but alien, she said, "You go on and think it over and come back after dark when they're home." She went inside quickly because he had touched some soft core and opened her and let out the true self—your arms could not gather back that sea—and she wanted to sit, spill, bask in that madness she was unaccustomed to, for she had walled it out. If anything, Kate would say, "Where'd you ever learn such control, Sis?" and sometimes Jarvis, "How'd we ever keep order in this house without you?" or even the children, "Mama never knows where things are."

Yes, where?

Now he waited outside the back door—he was infinitely polite—until she smiled and beckoned. He came in, wearing the brown alpine hat with the little gray feather he all but lived in. As always—he wouldn't intrude—he'd needed that second invitation to enter and sit at the other end of the table facing her and remove his hat and perch it on his knee, never elsewhere, always poised for flight. And as the days went, as she watched how the others were receiving him, registering how Ruthie and the girls warmed to him, even leaned toward him, though he would never reach out—he guarded his hands, she noticed—though he listened and laughed, which animated the kids in a new way: They opened up. Of the boys, it was Dennie, a constant competitor, who respected him: "Random goes—you should see him, Lib—lickety-split. All you hear's plop-plop-plop. He's got a rhythm." And maybe Llewelyn's increasing consciousness of his fat made him sit always closest to Random, as if he understood an ally. But big as Random was, it was Travis who *would* be met in combat, gymnastics, mock fights, boxing— "*You* can hold me over your head, Random, or flip me. Look." They waited. But she caught the quick stir of Random's eyes, dartings—as, with finesse and what agility, he had turned slightly and his hands forking and dividing began to try to speak with all courtesy to his new boss. Now Jarvis would linger a bit awkwardly before going to bed. Was he warding off her chats with Random to protect her? to keep him from making a nuisance of himself? to be possessive about what was his? For Jarvis must have sensed how all day now she had begun to expect that moment when, the others gone to bed, Random would sit at the table with her, as now, for his coffee, and talk. Yes, talk. She was learning. His fingers rode and divided air, and the first perceptions, words, pierced her with such pleasure she'd smile or laugh softly not to wake anyone.

He had trimmed his mustache and beard neatly. His full firm lips, if wordless, conveyed meaning in the subtlest variety of smiles and movements when his fingers did not. She had acquired from will and desire and practice a growing vocabulary in his finger language to make him feel at home when he returned at night from scalloping. Words in motion added a new dimension—words became the flesh they were—and she kept a pad and pencil near so he could write words for the signs she couldn't capture. There were questions that with a kind of gentility (it *was* that) he evaded: All those years what was it like at home? Did you leave home early? Do you ever go back to see your people? Did they treat you well? Where did you go that year? She came to recognize the brief, almost imperceptible hesitations, the stillnesses in his soft brown eyes, a lowering of his long dark lashes, the abrupt smile as he fixed his eyes anew on her and, instead of answering, questioned about her mother, her childhood, the family, town.

But he was—it came—

"An orphan!"

He laughed. There are so many! He unfurled. It came—it grew, his life. He was from Alabama—yes, born there. His mother had died not long after. Of poverty—what else? Bad times in the county. He was put in a home. You went to school, lived in a ward, there was a woman keeper—he wrote it, *Mrs Tenniel*—and he worked in the fields, did chores. The fields, orphanage, animals surrounded her—she *saw*. And he went out on his own then? Yes. Had some college too. But could not bear *tied down*. Wanted to know and see—all. Maybe walls had held him too long. Someday he would go back down South for good. Alabama? Oh, yes. Roots, memories, sights—you can't remove them, can you? Somehow he would tell it, if he found the words. He laughed. His mouth rounded wide in perfect white teeth.

She saw the useless tongue so red, wet. She vibrated with that tongue till her own went dumb.

She dabbed marshmallow fluff into his coffee. He laughed.

At first, if he looked too long at her, she felt her own severe face, her father's square bones, the thick brows, even the tautness at her hairline from the weight of the drawn, heavy bun. But she had learned to yield, for she knew—as she had known the day of his arrival—he had seen; there was no veil over his eyes, and flesh was no veil. He knew, but not specifics, it would seem; and it remained for his hands, yes hands, to draw out her life so in some way he could finger it, fondle the facts that were the signs of a facade that he could penetrate to what was true.

And you? Tell me you. Why you never married, he said.

This time her hands rose in a gesture futile—and she drew them back, for they were worn and harsh, bigger than she'd have them, they took the grace from her slim and firm body.

Because you seem so much a girl, young.

Her youth palpitated. "But I'm fifty," she said.

You weren't always. He laughed at his own play.

So each night, if she had begun the journey, this night she approached the source (the fire that a woman knew she would know, that would break all limits of flesh, so she could go on with that or the memory of it for as long as she would *be*).

"I am where I have always been. I have never been anywhere else. My father owned rich land, a large farm, had two daughters, Kate and me, and when my mother died I was eighteen, Kate eight, then *he* died so the lot fell to me. Kate married Jarvis when she was eighteen and took her part of what my father had left. She was sick after Dennie was born—sick a year—and Jarvis thought he'd get rich in a hurry, so speculated and lost. I was taking care of Kate but lived at home, so not, it will surprise you, lonely because . . . ."

Because.

Not lonely was the part, if not fully confirmed, he had entered—her world of the still grasshopper, water, a fish, cloud—hers whether from long stillness, isolation, suffering, or her own nature. But a time comes when you want to be absolutely apart and yet become the earth too and sky and sea and move with the wind. For this, she could not find fingers, or say, or even write the right words, but he said:

Who was he?

"To help in what way I could, I decided to sell the farm and move in with them—Kate and Jarvis and Dennie, who was by now, it seemed, my own. The man who came, the buyer, was young and very big, strong, broad, dark, first generation from Poland, with the pitch brown eyes so usual in Poles, deep, and hands that you knew could wield any plow, horse, earth. He did not buy the house."

She smiled and, if she did not move, she went from him and stayed for a time in that far moment.

All her life she would remember the barn, the wood wall and ground—and the burn of sun in that darkness—and a clutching and clutching to hold what was releasing her everywhere.

"No, he did not buy the house. He married me.

"And four months later was drowned in the Sound.

"And what was left was a miscarriage."

How could she say: He released me, the animal in him crucified and crucified, but he held himself from the world (he would roll over, ended).

Telling it, she saw the boy's eyes drift to whatever it was he was seeing, narrowing, perhaps with some pain in himself, some pity perhaps for her. She was glad for the stillness they had reached.

At night, after he had gone to bed in the back entry, having handed her the clothes, she put them through the washer-dryer. She touched the clean clothes. She wondered when last somebody had touched what he wore.

What else could she give?

She dared not ask Jarvis how long he could stay.

But Jarvis said, "Oh, he works hard—steady, you wouldn't believe, you'd think the job all depended on him, he was born to it." She feared that *Oh* and that *all*. She knew Jarvis's chafes, though more days than before, he let two or three of the children, and once all of them, go to school—and stay. "Random makes up for all of us," Dennie said, though those nights they all opened the catch, and the work, if not the number of buckets, was short. You could not believe the time discipline saved.

Now the kids admired and imitated.

"But quiet without the kids," Jarvis confided. "I miss their voices."

Now as the kids worked, they told Random their day: A boy tried to burn the exams in a teacher's desk, bikers from the city were racing on the sand cliffs, Lee and his brother smoked pot, Miss Alberson was dating Mr Rhodes from the bank, Jimmie Beason started a fight in Miss Callan's room, we told a fib so we could go scalloping with you.

And Jarvis confided, if grudgingly, "They work good when he's there. I have to hand that to him."

She said, "I baked you your apple pie today." She would, in her sympathy, for a moment give him back Kate, knowing Random, gathering the children, was gathering Kate about him. Alone, Jarvis was afloat. And afraid—never more so when he saw the children were mastering signs, and with such speed they could speak *his* language, and laughed, belly-laughed, bellowed.

"Whyn't you get busy, you?" Jarvis would fling the shells hard, they'd clack or break.

But mornings, ready for the depot and the market, he was satisfied with the take. Even reduced by Random's share, the cash came to more than he'd made without him. And Random insisted half go back, for his keep. But she stood between. "I'll decide that." You had to remember, no matter who, that if it was Jarvis's house, she was the order. Though no words had ever spoken it, that was her silent condition since Kate's illness years gone. She would not change the way of a life.

For a minute now all the world, after a brief cool spell, was released to the stillness of October, the illusion of summer, that joyful deception of life in the red gold brown turning leaves before the great blows and abrupt cold and the threat of snow. In the yard in the mums with their violent yellow cries, the fall roses, the pungent marigolds, she recognized her own body. What you saw was the effect of the motion.

The flies thrived with a mad buzzing she herself felt in her blood, and on the fish stink that dripped from the burlap and baskets and buckets pungent with strong sea salt. The fragrances and the stench roused her to wander free of the house when the family was away—miles along the Sound shore and cliffs, past fields of dead potato plants, through the woods, past ponds and inlets.

On the bay side, she saw the men scalloping, pulling baskets, raking, netting—specks against the stretch of water and sky.

And one morning when she knew they were at Pete Neck, she would surprise them—she packed sandwiches, thermoses of hot coffee and chocolate, cake, and fruit in a knapsack and made the long hike. How she felt the earth meet her feet, the air liven her face, the sun stir her blood. She followed the isolated dirt road through sea grass twice her height, swaying deeps of gold, till she came to an inlet and shielding her eyes ranged till she found them and advanced to the edge and stood there drawing in the rank odor of mud flats baking in sun and the dank sea mixed with the dry wheat scent of sea grass making a clear dry rattle and chafe in the wind.

"Yooooooo." She flagged.

It was Llewellyn who bobbed in the water and cried the word to them. "It's Libby! Hey, you!" Dennie was rowing. Jarvis and Ruthie had rakes, and Dot and Random seemed to be dredging. It was some time before they drew together, piled all into the rowboat, and made their way toward the flats. She had spread a great plastic tablecloth and begun to lay out the food.

"Eats, kids," Jarvis said, and smiled. "You get lonesome?"

"I'd forgotten what Pete Neck looked like."

He went down on his knees, facing the water, flagging them in. "There'll be nothing left."

They removed their boots. "Ahhhh."

Llewellyn grabbed a sandwich and fell on his back, a mound. They were an octopus, scooping up sandwiches, paper cups, pickles—

"You'll *choke*, Ruthie."

But it was Dot who gasped, "Pa!" She was struggling and signaling. "Random!" Sudden as the word, he was gone.

Lib made to shout, her throat caught, but her arm flagged madly. She knew how water could end you.

They all turned and stared an instant before Dennie leaped, calling, "Random Random Random," and strode in. Llewellyn splashed after, then Dot and Ruthie, close, as if fear made them one.

"There he is!" she cried. Random came up as quickly as he had vanished, flailing against the water, but choked and coughed and could not stand—he went flat. They saw the bulk of Jarvis's jacket Random was wearing. "His clothes're soaked. Jarvis, he'll drown."

Why didn't he move?

"Jarvis!"

"Not in such shallows," Jarvis said, but moved.

Random caught footing and staggered and swayed. His arms groped at the air, and he stood. She herself was in the water, moving faster than she knew she could, her dress clinging and pulling. All her flesh was crying out against the water.

"Don't *you* drown!" Jarvis was beside her.

Llewellyn, for all his weight, came up first beside Random, and Dennie fast after. They reached out to help him. Dot said, "Let me." Ruthie, crying, could only say, "Random, Random."

But Random's arms made spasms, and he staggered from them, his mouth wide as if he would speak. Lib saw it was fear. She shouted in a pitch she almost never used, in fear for him, "Stop! Stop! He's all right." As fast as she said it, they halted, bewildered. "He's fine. Let him stand." They saw then he was, he had gathered himself, he was shaking his head at his own stupidity. Now he smiled, relieved, and *they* laughed loud, nervous.

"Wow! You sure scared us," Llewellyn said. "Come on, let's eat."

And Random was explaining. His hands made a dip, a sink: He'd lost balance, went under, choked.

"You get those sinks sometimes," she said, but she was watching Jarvis, some shame before her, and she dropped her eyes at that blight, feeling his shame, if even some pity.

Random sat and was quietly regaining air in deep breaths. She knew nobody could touch him. She throbbed with the pain of whatever hurts he had once known.

"Now you all take your time eating."

"Look at you, you're soaked, Lib," Jarvis said. Clothes were her skin; she could be naked.

Her shadow fell over him and he looked up quickly when she did not move, but to assure, she moved off and sat.

"There!" She let out an assault of hard rock. "I brought your transistor, Dennie."

"We won't be resting that long," Jarvis said.

That night the voices were loud and happy as family in the cellar. They were all adept now, fingers flew. Only Jarvis, his eyes on the knife, resisted Random's silent language, isolated by their laughter and curiosity and agility in learning. "Dad, you know what he's saying?" "I guess I can guess," Jarvis said. "And what's this, summer vacation?" he said, and "You're not slumming down Park Avenue, you know." But nothing could speak so loudly as Random's constancy with the knife, as he whipped whipped whipped mussel after mussel out of the scallop shells plop plop plop in the bucket. But when a new silence settled, he said, "Cat got your tongues?" He grunted, scowling his *never-enough* scowl at the number of gallons of scallops, though the truth was there were more than ever.

Deep into one Sunday morning, after an especially lucky day, after he'd put the cellar light out and they'd all gone up to bed and Random was drinking his coffee, Jarvis said, "Ruthie and Dot are getting especially tired. I'm keeping them out of school too much. Maybe Dennie and Llewellyn can take off every other day from now on."

Did he mean Random was so fast he overwhelmed?

"Besides, the season's about over," Jarvis said.

Over? But it was nowhere into November, though with winter she'd be glad to be rid of the pervasive smell and the flies.

Did Random know?

But she guarded a silence.

"And I guess Kate wouldn't have wanted me to keep them out of school so much. . . ."

Kate. His words stood her there. She was somewhere in the house. Even Random seemed aware of a presence and with delicacy withdrew and shut the back door. You could hear him slip from his clothes, then the cot creak.

She herself might have lain down.

All that night Kate whispered, and her Pole, and the voice she had conceived for Random and never heard. When she woke, thinking *cellar*, there were no voices, but a face, and she knew he must be lying in the hall, not asleep now, and seeing her own face.

But when, on the Tuesday following, over his coffee Random told her (he had outsat Jarvis), I'll be going, I'll tell him tomorrow, her own voice choked back mute. He sat particularly long. She knew it was his gift to her, that they could sit together and listen to the silence that they were, which would move and move, and forever.

The next night they all sat up late after they had opened all the scallops. Dennie sulked. "You're hardheaded. You could stay." His voice tremored. Llewellyn, never still a minute, was still—and bit out "Bye" and stomped up the stairs. Only Dot said, "You could have warned us. You could have told us, you!" And Ruthie said, "You'll come back, won't you?" But he wouldn't lie. And Dot cried openly and clung to Lib. Random clutched his hands. He would not touch, or let touch? And, thanks to Jarvis's "Get yourselves to bed," it ended.

Jarvis made sure Random had his pay. And went up.

She washed the cups and glasses while Random sat there. In the pane she saw her face and again that face that had come to her.

She said, "You must rest," and went to her room.

Where all the night she lay awake, and heard.

In the morning she slipped out of bed and into her clothes, and wrapped the hair she'd let down and washed, and went in for her frying pan—and then opened the entry door.

He was always up first, and waiting.

So he was gone, the bedding and cot folded, the boots set out, the borrowed clothes hung—all ordered. And the knapsack gone.

Jarvis said, "Get the kids up. I'll need them all today." Was that his concession to how much work Random could do. He would go directly to gather the equipment, but she said, "You eat your breakfast."

And when they had all gone, too silent and solemn, into the warm of morning, she did the dishes but did not wait to face that window that had become more than a view that changed with the seasons. It held him, and permanently, she feared. On impulse, because a warm wind was already stirring the kitchen curtains, she went outside to stand where he had stood, and looked in as he had looked in at her in that window, and then went into the depleted garden, where the mums burned yellow and brown with morning sun, their scent strong and searing, and she went on her knees and pulled around them as if it were not coming winter and not useless, but feeling the strength in her fingers, her lungs. She sweat, all her skin and scalp, till her back and head felt the sun deep and she stood with a reeling, and laughed, fingering wind. She felt damp under her breasts, sticky, her dress wet, back and armpits. And so inviting was the wind, easy the blow, she went up the street and crossed the back road to the fields, all a warm rising from the ground. Her feet made loud clear flicks against the fallen potato plants and kicked clumps of dried sod. She walked to the Sound cliffs and descended to the beach. All was balm, a breeze that pressed and whispered. She walked the strip of white stones, they made a hard grind and echoed in a hard scraping. The Sound hardly moved in vague slumps and swells like skin over deep breaths, making the softest hush.

She went straight toward the clusters of boulders. From the work and the walk her skin and scalp prickled, but the beach lured and her body yearned to keep moving. She bent to test the water—cold, but it livened—and when she stood and leaned, so much warmth came from the boulder, evoking such desire, that she went between the great rocks, completely hidden from view, and undressed. She would go in naked, swim till the cold water answered her live flesh. She stood, letting the sun seep into her, raised her arms to the warm air, exulting—and stepped in. Yes, cold! If the air was summer, winter waited in the water. The ledges were sudden drops, first clear white stones, then seaweed and rocks, then the drop into darkness. She went in to her knees and stopped, peering under: There, still as a rock, lay a great skate, motionless over the white stones. She stared long at it: the great graceful spread of its fins, like wings, the narrowing to a long still tail like a spear. It lay like a man with his forearms folded under, elbows out.

She stepped in to her waist. The skate did not move. When she waded deeper, it made the slightest, almost imperceptible undulation forward—she smiled at its almost magical movement—and went under. The skate glided below her, directly under, as she rode down over the seaweed and rocks barnacled and fringed with green. She came up for breath and went down again. It was there—as if waiting, white as she in the deeps. It moved, and she moved, she rose and it rose, her body thrust in long clean sweeps and it undulated, and as she turned it rose over and she saw its dark shadow under sun and then it went down, a white shadow in the dark below. She struggled down until all she felt was the rhythm of the great white and dark shadows they became, moving over long angles of seaweed and down over ledges into the gray dark, and hovered before the invisible dark ahead. For a long moment she stared at the glint of the eyes in its back till it seemed there was no motion. The skate broke the stillness; it edged into the dark and stilled. She moved only the slightest, exulting in this perfect balance. Then it went—into true dark. She could see nothing. But she felt its presence there in the dark. For a fraction of a second she yearned to go farther. But her blood was beating in the silence and her lungs yearned for breath—she would break. And she thrust upward, her legs churning, her arms in great wheelings upward, and the light grew and it veered till she burst into air and sun and her lungs gasped and sucked.

Rocks and sand and cliffs and the far trees and sky stood stark, each burning with its own color.

She reached shore, her flesh numb, yet she felt raw alive, the sand and sky and boulders pulsed, and for a moment she had to lean against a boulder, letting the heat slowly fuse into her before she came fully to and realized she must dress, thinking, *He's up there somewhere watching*, and she wondered in whose body she was walking.

She was halfway up the beach when she saw him and halted. He was deep in shrubs on the high edge of the cliff.

But—

It was Jarvis!

She hurried, though he did not move.

"The kids! Something happened?"

Because he looked stricken. Or guilty.

"Nothing. I just had a feeling . . . ."

"Feeling?"

"I thought I was right—because the house was empty."

She led the way across the dry field. "You're a fool, Jarvis."

"You might have gone . . . somewhere."

"And what would the kids do?"

"Kids—"

"My kids," she said. "You know what I stay for."

"Something could change your mind."

What she heard was a question.

"Nothing. Nobody."

"You've never gone before. You might want to."

She halted, nearly drugged by the scent of pine and dry earth and by the warm air touching and teeming. Then she headed home. And not looking back, she murmured, "Where would I go, Jarvis?"

MINOR MATTERS

(Of Lust, Gluttony, Avarice, Sloth, Wrath, Envy, Pride, and Other Minor Matters)

That Unforgettable Day

"This is the worst day of my life, Sue," he said. She didn't know. She couldn't know or she wouldn't for a minute think of leaving him. But even as he said what he had so often thought, feeling violent, thinking *beat, kill, die, commit suicide*, he knew what somehow he had dreaded for months had happened at last—her saying it was almost a relief, but a relief too terrible, the sudden fall of a wall that opened onto meaningless space, an endless blank future. He wanted to say—he did say it to himself as he had said it the day he had come home from the physical exam—"I can't help it." He was sterile. For two years they'd been as happy as any couple alive, hadn't they? Then, fairly comfortably *fixed*, both had wanted a baby, and desperately. After a year of trying, frustrated, fearing a possible truth—who perhaps was *to blame*?—Christ, how he hated that day!—she'd gone to Doctor Falk—"I'm fine"—and then *he'd* gone. It was the darkest day, life turned dark, the future went black. He might have been blind.

And then he did not believe it. He would prove Falk wrong. He was constantly at her, going at it with insatiable lust, yearning, dreaming, praying. But nothing. Nothing! After each madness, each of her infallible periods, he wanted to cry, rail—at himself, *himself*, at genes, parents, nature, God. He was wearing her down, her patience, endurance, sympathy. He knew that. He knew from her quiet innuendoes—her drifting from him in conversation, staring; her sometimes passive fierceness in sex, a feigning, or sometimes an exertion that he was sure came from pity, which he did not, did *not*, want. At such instants, out of sheer guilt he wanted to strike her, though he was aware that it was himself he wanted to strike. And he could not conceal from himself that he was biding his time, waiting for some judgment: because she had taken to living a private inner life—in some way he no longer existed for her.

"But you love me," he said. "You *do*, don't you?"

"Yes," she said but her tone was heavy with reserve. And after one irritable, tense argument, knowing as always the cause was sex, *baby*, she said, "Yes, I do love you, but sometimes love is not enough, you can't live with love alone. I can't. I want what's in me. I want to be fulfilled. I want to give my life to what's in me. That's love too. Can't you understand that?"

"*Yes*. You know I can. But we could adopt," he said, fearful of losing her. "There're babies. After all, it's what you bring up as yours that you love." He reasoned that, he knew it was true, but he did not feel it. He was lying: Because more than anything *he* too wanted what was in him, the line, them, what he carried. But he did *not* carry it. And she *did*.

She was crying. She didn't want to do this to him—he knew that—she felt compelled to—he knew that, understood that—and though the moment she'd said it he had hated her, when he saw her sitting there crying, alone—yes, alone in ways he himself had come to despise being alone—he felt sorry for her, he felt sorry because she wanted what *he* wanted and he wanted her to have it, but what smote day and night, what lacerated when he thought, was that he could not give her or himself what they both wanted.

"I can't," he murmured. "I wish I could, but I can't."

And for a minute he loathed her again when she said, "But, Brooks, I can," though his loathing was a confused mingling of resentment and desire and hurt and love that left him helpless.

So, helpless, after the sale of the house and the divorce and division of possessions, in a deathly numbness, he, this genius of laser medical technology who couldn't even penetrate his wife successfully, arranged for a short escape before a transfer to Chicago to continue his work in conjunction with doctors from the team under Germond at the Vaud University Hospital Center in Switzerland, shocking Professor Johnson at the local loss of their "brightest light." "You knocked the legs right out from under me," Johnson said. He left Johns Hopkins and went back north to his parents' house in the village on Long Island to settle with himself, feeling like the simplest of criminals escaping to the farthest point he could from the crime.

Making the Rounds

He had not told his parents *sterile*, told them only *incompatible*, whatever *doubt* their faces showed. "You've got to keep your mind up," his father said. "And your body, don't forget that," his mother said. He couldn't stop thinking *And not* your *faces, bodies, minds?* because he saw them reproduced and reproduced. His mother saw to it he didn't forget his body, knowing that in bad moments one compensates: He had forgotten how great old-fashioned home cooking could be. And she half did it, he was certain, to try to keep him home. She and his father hated the meanness of smalltown talk. "We don't see much of you," she said, not to accuse but with maternal longing. No TV evenings for *him*, he thought, but said, "I didn't realize how many of my old high school friends hadn't left town." "So I've noticed," she said. He laughed. "You're a killer, Ma." But the real killers—he hoped so—were Rhoda, Dottie, Vince, Willis, Randy Owen, Marsha, Lydia from next door, the three Walsh girls, Gwen. God, when he thought, if he spent half his time in The Tavern, in and out of The Barge and Porky's and the Elbow Inn and Sound View, he spent the rest of it shacking up, half the time in the back seat of the car. At first it was "Jesus, *Louise*! *You* here!" thrilled, startled at the sudden *boy* he felt, something was happening, you could repeat night after night the same startle, the same joy, with somebody else. But at repeats the joy fizzled: Drinks made the faces saviors, softened the dark, till times when he'd reach the point where an invisible layer was peeled off his eyes and abruptly he saw the pores in the skin, pimples, mucous, wet rictuses so clearly that he backed off—it was all *tits* and *cunt, fucking*, and *How's yours?* and empty kisses and empty passion, *You satisfied? It was great, doll, great. We'll do it again sometime.* And Ma never complained he reeked, his breath, his clothes, his car, but said, "Have you been to the Sound or Gull Pond? You used to love to swim." And row. And fish. And crab. And and and. His father was more direct, but diplomatic. "We could both do with a good workout." "I'm having one," he said. His father smiled wryly. "You might go out in the boat with me one day. It's great exercise." "I might do that." But he didn't miss his father's scrutiny. Behind him, he saw himself in the mirror. He saw the evidence of his nights and days. Who was all that? That gut. Thirty days that shook the world! Laugh. Swim it off.

Swimming with the Dead

The great boulders were like prehistoric creatures resting dormant on the beach, the sand struck almost yellow by sun, the rib of pure white stones as far as the eye could see along the shore. His impulse to swim was so strong. All the day heralded it. A pre-summer sun made great green inviting streaks of clarity in the water—he stripped—there was no one on the beach, only one house in sight, the Brandons' redwood on the cliff, always closed till true summer—and left his clothes in plain sight at the foot of the boulder that towered over his head. *Into these waters*. He dived in, struck cold, seeing clear his way among the boulders, between diminishing darks that seemed to quiver with fine green algae. The ledges down were abrupt and sharply clear, the bottom laden with seaweed brown and long whose tentacles he rode over, into, hardly feeling their chafing. He let his weight take him down, gliding into the increasing dark. Deeper, he had to exert his arms and legs to keep him down and guide his body past now glimpses of white, wriggles of white, phantoms that at once vanished into the gray above or dark below. Now he saw only his arms' vague white motions and caught ghostly glimpses of his legs. He turned numb, all his body numb—glad to fuse with this cold and dark, to *be* cold and dark, not feel, to feel nothing, leave it all there above the surface—sun, green, home, town, Sue—stop that motion for this, this. Only his arms, feebly, moved, only his thought he could not stop. Wasn't all this fertility there in his thinking? Let the other present cease moving. Let only this, this residue, remain—and *no, not even that* to cling to. Drift in this current. Sink down, down into silt, still, where it was too deep even for the current to stir it. *That.* It was all so lightning quick his thought that he hardly realized how taut his limbs grew, how they seemed even to have vanished. In an almost frenzy he thought *This. Yes. Dare. Stillness. Now. Forever.* His arms tried to force him down—deep, deep. But his chest ached, his lungs cried out *against*, like electric in him—his body yearned to rise. But white approached—what fish, white? a skate?—and, behind, others—But no, not a skate. Even now his mind numbed at the sight but all his body took sudden fear—a *face*, his *brother's* face. Almost he opened his mouth to shout *Al*, but Al's face flushed almost against his, and vanished, and others came: Uncle Eldridge drowned in the war, his neighbor Loretta found fallen off Preston's dock, drunk Clarence Wilson dumped in the harbor after foul play, Eddie his stepfather and uncle Dan drowned when a storm came up as they were trying out a rowboat they'd built, the seven Polack fishermen whose fishing boat sank off Montauk, Johnny Gates who fell and struck his head on the rowboat and went under—and faces from the town's war-drowned and faces from the photos in the family album and then imagined from all the tales told him by aunts, parents, grandparents, relatives, townspeople. They surrounded him. He turned and turned. They were everywhere, alive, moving, and he was *with* them. He wanted them to take him wherever they were going. He extended his arms to them. He moved—he had to—his lungs would burst, the pain was sharp; but he wanted them, they were his. Yet his body yearned against all his desire. *Come!* He thrust his arms out to draw them all up together. But he tore through their faces, they dissolved, and at their going he burst into air, light, sun with a painful cry over the water where there was nothing, nobody to hear him.

Genius at Work

But somebody he wanted, he had to have, and if not somebody, work. The madness of sex and food that merely disguised solitude was not for him. Drown in work. My salvation, work. He went to Chicago. Half a country from Sue. He couldn't resist writing, though she'd sent back the four letters mailed to her father's address. *I don't want to give you false hope,* she'd written on the first one, *so please don't write, please.* He knuckled down, boned in. "Don't you ever go home nights? Trying to kill yourself?" Sheryl said. She was the perfect assistant, quiet, meticulous, understanding, who never nosed into the personal but let him talk at will. She had a severe Southern blonde beauty, scant makeup, trim ponytail, and, what he liked most, always wore a dress. She was one of three sisters living together who had no intention of marrying, she said, unless a miracle. . . . She grew on him. When she was not there and he stopped work, exhausted, wanting breath, words, perfume, chafings, he felt that going out for a quickie violated something between them, better to masturbate, which he did profusely until a weekend when her sisters were going away. "Come over for a drink?" He had never known anything like her: She was an experienced artist at it, her body beautiful, more beautiful in motion. She mounted and—astride, absolutely in control—managed to hold him in her but hold him off through waves of ecstasy. She was a revelation. He had never known such pleasure. After, it became obsessive. Often noons they took a room for a quick hour at the nearby Holiday Inn. He marveled. She was insatiable. But at the lab she was never intimate, though they were a perfect team. The affair went on for two years. By then Sheryl knew more about him than he could tell, but not his nightmares of pits, black, labyrinths to dead ends; not his dreams of semen bursting into flower, semen implanted and ejected, semen made fertile, incredible pills, capsules, liquid injections; of reverse growth, back to the womb to be reborn with the creatures ready and waiting in him. And if Sheryl did not pall, the thought of the dead end of their pleasure did. Day after day the futile cycle. The one thing she did not understand was his frenzy for work—for money? Oh, he had piled it up, wanted it, someday it would serve . . . when he knew for what, how. But, no, not money. He dreamed *babies*, dreamed *fertility*, dreamed—he could never escape the dream—of hoards of men and women marching on him, crying out for help. He knew it was an obsession, but he could not stop the dream. Sometimes in dreams he saw Sue naked with her legs spread wide and tiny creatures emerging one after the other, endlessly. He realized he had to put an end to the nightmares, pursue the dream; but the first step was to break this mould. What would follow? Reduce yourself, he said. Get to rock bottom. Begin. Think. Take your chances. And abruptly one day he decided to appeal for a transfer to Madrid to work with Pérez his old colleague and a close associate of Germond. Sheryl was deeply moved. She cried, but he knew it was for the loss of habit, a need, and even a long-time affection, but not love. Later she kidded. "Did you think I'd propose to you to keep you here? No go! I haven't changed my mind about marriage." "But you can have kids." "Who wants them!" Nothing she had ever said reduced him to such despair. That night he dreamed the silent horde was marching down on him. When he managed to struggle out of the dream, for some minutes he was sure those creatures were standing there in the dark, surrounding him.

In a Foreign City

He was tired. Why tired? This busy little barrio he had settled in—old, picturesque, Bohemian with windows overlooking the Lavapies plaza—all too quickly had lulled him to its rhythm. The first few days he visited the Prado, churches, museums; explored for choice restaurants; took the Metro to its last stops and wandered the barrios. Soon he was going down to the street and sitting on the plaza, watching neighbors, tourists, and immigrants over coffee from the Salón Recreativo or after four and into morning sitting among the noisy spontaneous night Bohemians in the Nuevo Barbieri, where—he liked to tease Rosario—she had "accosted" him. "But you were too willing—and we *had* spoken in the hallway," which now meant he had let himself slip into a relationship. She was slim and dark, energetic and untiring—passionate: And once she had become familiar with his apartment, she one day invaded and cleaned it from top to bottom. "Your bid for a relationship?" She laughed. "It *would* be cheaper for both of us." Before and after work at the photography office not far off, in Sol, she did all she could for his comfort. He eased into it, sank, fascinated by the miniature world of the barrio, among the familiars. He watched the kids, numerous, play at football, climb, fight; watched till he could identify by their cries Jesús, Juan, Angel, Carlitos, Ramón, Norberto, Rubén . . . But what drew and held him and provoked were the addicts huddled between autos, in doorways and alleys, *pinchándose*; the prostitutes, especially the old ones, standing on corners, tireless in their worn clothes with their *bolsas* hanging from their shoulders, their dyed hair flagrantly faded; the pervasive odor of *mierda* dropped by dogs and urine from kids and old men pissing in any spot when the spirit moved; and the constant shrieks and cries that died down at three for meals and siesta. What surprised—startled—him was that he did not condemn them; he watched with curiosity, with a suspension of all moral judgment. It was their life. They chose it. He looked on. He felt like a mirror collecting flat images with an illusion of depth, just as, he realized, he was the all-nighter at the Barbieri or with Rosario detached even in the act of sex. He might have been viewing a film in which he was the protagonist, observing without reacting, without being moved, feeling nothing his own self was feeling in the film. At times aware that he was inhabiting the space, a void, between his actual body and whatever he was watching, himself or others, his mind would probe—Why?—but he felt no pain, no conscience, no sense of the emotional worry or terror which he knew he *ought* to be feeling. How was he different at such moments from those *drogadictos*? He was as much like them as he was different from the beggars and the old people sitting on benches on the plaza talking or reading the paper because they were—surely they *felt*—responsible to the motion around him in which they were as solid as he was drifting in it.

So when Rosario insisted he watch the Easter processions—"You can't be in Madrid at *Pascua* and not see them" (she was standing in the hallways on his landing, dressed for Mass)—he said, "Why not?," drifting. He went through the last days of Christ as the events were depicted on those great floats carried through the street with women dressed in black and barefooted and dragging chains tied to their ankles, the crowds silent. He was *stirred.* Rosario, sensing his emotion, said, "You see. I told you you would be moved by this tragedy." "Moved, yes." He was startled. This was the first time since his arrival that he *felt.* He had crossed some void. Now there was no distance between him and that man crucified, but she did not understand. *Sympathy*, she must be thinking. But it was antipathy. He hated it—he felt the violence of his own fury directed at that crucified man—because he was dead before his time and not, no, having wanted to die—even at that last minute wanting *for that instant* nothing but to live. A weak moment? How could anybody say that? Didn't they see his tragedy? Jesus wanted to live, but did *not* live. A thirty-three year old man—with no woman. What good did it do to wash a prostitute's feet? Cleanse? Reduce him to humility? To *know* a woman? And what was humility—no sex, no body, death—but to *know* a woman? And what was that if it did not mean to know what passed through them like electricity, known but unknown, creating you but not you, to see it in the new body, that new you not you, the child, and so *more* you. And if you did not—or could not—do that, then dead *here* or dead *there* did not matter because the one consolation would be that that motion would go on and on *here* in something that moved if even in stillness, stone, son. So that now for an instant wanting this and at the same moment confessing *for that instant* that his vision of some continuity *elsewhere* and *preferable*, failed, showing the crucified man's humanity, only his humanity, nothing more. His humanity. *Mine.* Without that fabricated illusion. Naked. Alone. To face only what was in him, afraid of what was in him. Cut off from what he most desired. So he—though he could not explain it all to Rosario—he could not hide his anger or his anguish—but he said, "What good could he do but affirm this life?" Rosario said, "He saves us. Don't you see that?" "Saves you?" "Yes. He offers us— Don't you want eternal life?" "I don't want to die for it." "We might die—but don't: we live *there*." He was silent. "So you didn't appreciate what you saw. I'm sorry." She was really disturbed. She withdrew, perhaps deep into the emotion of her faith. He wanted to tell her his anger was directed not at that man he saw represented there but at himself for *his* inadequacies. That night he went up to her *piso*. "I'm sorry, I'm sorry, I'm truly sorry, Rosario," he said. "You helped me. The procession did. It really did." He kissed her, thinking of the Judas kiss, but it was a kiss of genuine consolation because it affirmed his life with her, the body. But he did not say that. She had broken the distance between him and her, him and another. He felt. He was roused from that long lethargy. He wanted to live.

A Glimpse of Hell

At the screams that would not stop, Rosario said, "It's Ana, little Ana."

He rushed out into the hall.

"Diego and Elena fighting again!" she cried. But this time it was really *un escándalo*— screams, shouts, thuds. And in a moment there was Rosarios's pounding on Elena's door.

"Elena, *querida*, what? *what?*" She doubled the pounding but the ruckus inside did not cease. "Elena! Diego!"

Then came a sudden silence.

"What, Rosario?" Mark said.

They stood in the corridor, waiting. For a long time there was no movement inside. not a sound.

Rosario struck the door with the flat of her hands.

"Elena, *abre! Abre, por favor!*"

There were murmurs, sounds of pleading, muffled crying.

"Elena?"

"*Vete*, Rosario," Elena said. "Go."

It was two days before they herd anyone come out of the apartment.

It was Ana.

Downstairs, outside on the sidewalk, she had taken a shine to him. Four she was. Ana, Elena's little girl. Elena lived with her man Diego on Rosario's floor. *Ana.* He had coddled her, surprising her with *Which hand?* for candy, sometimes a ribbon that Rosario or he himself would make into a bow; and one day with Elena's permission he took her to the zoo at Casa de Campo with Diego shouting down the stairs after her.

"The man hates her," Rosario said, "because she keeps Elena in Madrid. He's always wanting to haul her off to Barcelona, where he says they can make easy money—or *she* can, he means—but she wants him to work so she can give up her job. As it is, he lives on her, the bastard."

Mark and Ana had spent the day at the zoo. She came back with animals in her head, talking *monkeys, snakes*, teaching him words and words. But it was on the bus, on the way back to the Plaza de Isabel II—with Ana exhausted, almost asleep on his lap, huddled against him, his chin resting on her head, smelling the oil in her hair, not clean, with her withered dress and wasted shoes—that he felt he could sit this way, not move, sit holding her forever, warm, soft, her innocent neck fragile and quietly pulsing against his hand. And when he took her upstairs, it was Diego who opened the door, dark, a fury exiled in him, as always, who took her arm, drew her in and, silent, slammed the door. *Ana.* Who became his day. Mornings her shouts and laughter below on the sidewalk. Her steps, light, faltering sometimes, in the hall. Her cries, unbidden from behind that door, painful in him. Ana. Whom he came to expect. Who sought him. Who leaped over his legs, into his arms. "*Ay de mí!* How she loves you," Elena said, "because you spoil her. So *mimada*, that child. You want her, don't you?" She'd laugh. "I mean it. You want her?" And it was Rosario who said, "I'd like to think she was joking, but if I know half, Diego despises Ana." "How could he hate a child?" "How!" Rosario said. "Because he's *egoísta, puro egoísta*. "And, terrible as it is to say, I believe Elena'd give Ana up if she had to choose between her and Diego." "She'd be insane to!" "Who said she was sane? The world's full of insanity. Ask *her*, why don't you?" Though she was being rhetorical, as the weeks went and there were screams and crying, intermittent but constantly intermittent, he felt he did want to ask; and Ana's increasing play with him, spotting him, taking his hand, pulling at him, and on his lap tousling and touching made him feel *father* and *Sue* and *sterile* and *What death?* Made him long, desire. And sometimes dream *Sue*, dream *Ana*, dream *Sue-Ana-Mark*. In dreams he saw Sue with them here on the plaza, at the zoo, in the Lai-Lai restaurant below; Ana manipulating chopsticks; Ana by the lake at the Retiro with ice cream, in a rowboat with him and Sue.

So he woke that morning to terrible screaming—all the building woke to it, all four storeys—coming from Elena's; but when all the *Comunidad* crowded at the door, it was finally *Váyanse! Váyanse!*" from Diego. And when all day, all the next, no one came out, the president of the community knocked and knocked; and the others—disturbed, fearful, prescient—called the police and in no time came sirens, lights, battering.

Ana had been beaten to death by Diego—and with her mother standing there not raising a hand, a voice, *Jesus!*, like letting him beat *her*, Elena, because wasn't *she* Ana? *Wasn't* she? Or was he, Mark, insane, incapable of thinking or feeling? Was there some irrational psychology that evaded him completely? Because now—Ana! little Ana! *his* little Ana—because *wasn't* she *his* too now? That! That above all. He could not even imagine when he read 500 dead or 2,000 Tutsis Pakistanis Japs Germans Brazilian Indians or thought six million Jews, could not imagine thousands dead in hurricanes, earthquakes, tornadoes because you had to *see*—it was beyond visual imagination—but *one* made you see, one Ana made you see all, all, imagine, *imagine*. And now *he*, yes, *he* (his first reaction, feeling, thought, articulated) *he* was the word *kill*, he was *I could kill Diego*, and so now fury, fury, nearly absolute fury because he could not move, could not move to kill Diego. Diego had been taken at once, with Elena, surrendered, confessed—they had not run, had confessed—

"Why, Rosario? Rosario, why?"

"Because she loved Diego too much, more than Ana."

"Loved?"

"Wanted, then, more than she wanted Ana. Desired Diego, crazy with passion."

"Lost, you mean, in her passion."

"That. It's too terrible even to think it, but how do you stop thinking it?"

"How?" he said.

Ana.

He himself was *running*, was the little legs, the wasted shoes, her black long hair leaping. And arms, the mouth laughing, tiny white teeth flashing, the little red tongue.

He heard laughter, shouts of joy, cries, the high fine voice.

And then *nothing*.

On the stairway. On the plaza. Nothing.

Nowhere.

It made him—Rosario too—sick, days sick, though of course—what could you do?—they worked. At work he felt divorced—abstracted, *ensimismado* his colleagues said. Yes. *Pasará.* Like everything else, it will go, yes. Whenever he thought *Ana*, his fury returned. What kind of fury was in Diego if this was his own fury? But his fury subsided, that too passed. Even fury passed. But not Ana passed. What stayed was *his*. Ana was his now. She had been then too, he realized. It was the wonder-terror. Diego had killed. Diego had taken not only what was theirs but what was his.

Sue. If she knew! But she did not—she knew what was hers, only hers. She would have hers. He understood. She wanted hers, from her own body. Hers.

The Alien Guest

So now he became the guest, frequently, really the alien guest of his fellow employers (the Americans first, then English, Germans, finally Spaniards, always slow to take foreigners into their homes) because, of course, he was a catch (very available, most eligible, one of those choice American divorced, and, they made no bones about it, "brilliant," not only "there" but already on the way to a flowering in-house renown as modifications in surgery technology were adopted).

Though his barrio was picturesque, quiet, and quaint (quaint? drug addicts, beggars, illegals, a virtual UN of nationalities), the hierarchy and his colleagues (subtly?) suggested other barrios (pamphlets forgotten on his desk, quick "unintentional" tours, comments on one of the "places" to live) and even lured with guests (daughters, divorced women or professionals engaged in similar work in other companies) invited from barrios he would be "comfortable in." So from the houses and apartments *exquisiteces* from the Castellana to the other side of the Casa de Campo and as far out as San Agustín de Guadalix, he came to see *life*, they said, the best of Madrid.

It was Pérez with whom he renewed work and whom he liked most, this immediate associate meticulous in every detail, whose knowledge of latest medical equipment advances was impeccable. Like the best of the brilliant he was adventurous but reserved, desiring exhaustive medical completness before making judgments. He had come to trust Pérez and his results, and both the Swiss and Lausanne medical teams called them both in for exhaustive laser demonstrations on fecundation in vitro, his own obsessive concern, and they had succeeded in perforating the *zona pellucida* of the embryo and freed the cells to continue developing. It was the world's first use of this type of laser with no necesssity to touch or manipulate the ovule, with safety and with no secondary effects.

And his trust of Pérez extended to his personal life.

Pérez said, "So you won't yield to them? Why not let them latch you into the happiest of disasters? What else is marriage? Or, after a divorce, do you prefer the most disastrous happiness, single bliss, something, I have to add, we all—at times, and some not *only* at times—envy you."

"Well, that's a great reversal."

Pérez laughed. "No reversal at all. Why do you think they want to see you in the same state? Doesn=t every married man sometimes envy independence? Didn't you?"

"Sometimes. But then almost immediately I missed being tied down, a state—alas—most people desire after all."

But he was amused, a little flattered, and somewhat annoyed with his colleagues, and with himself for his reactions.

What they could not know was the cause of his own envy.

They invited him home. For cocktails. Dinner. The pool. To dances. But the intimate and unintended moments held him—the children rushing out to meet *Papi! Papi!*, the eruption of children's voices, the streak down the steps to the car, the kisses, the boy taking his hand, the girl carried—or between moments, their cries on the lawn, the games, the giggles and laughs upstairs, the *Excuse me, I must say goodnight to the children.*

And *sometimes* there were the moments, almost sacred to him, when the children came to him, offered him a tennis racket. *Venga.* And he played. Or one crawled up into his lap. Or always the wonderful moment he awaited, always in this country, the moment before the children must leave and each would kiss both his cheeks, the warm breath, damp lips, their sound trembling his marrow before they slipped off; and he would go home heavy with his envy and his own emptiness, wanting to be filled by them.

The teams verified that the new technique had produced pregnancies, though they were cautious in their predictions. What excited him and Pérez was that the laser-guaranteed security and avoided side effects. His part in the project since Sue was achieving results.

"It's a masterful achievement," Pérez said. "You must be proud."

"We. A lot of people went into this before it got to the doctors, and the technique is an easy one."

"But with your perception and—undeviating energy."

Undeviating? If Pérez knew!

"It could have been done much sooner. I think of the lives we missed saving."

After the first operation he was allowed in with the MDs to

see the patient. The miracle was that it was as if nothing had had to be done. Normal. The woman could live her life. She could breed.

"It could have been mine," he said.

But it was years too late.

"What?" Pérez said.

"Talking aloud," he said.

The team was highly lauded, the cases published in papers worldwide with the evident reservations. He felt pride, a good measure of pride, in his technological team, and in his own concentrated work. This. Born now, I could be this. And being lost in the transition and seeing himself as a victim of time and medical evolution, he had—he couldn't avoid it—a certain envy of that woman and the baby she would have, and of all women in whose uteruses transferred embryos might be implanted.

Newspaper publicity of the team's initial results brought him a letter from Sue, confessing her own pride in his contribution and reiterating the confidence that he would "go even further":

and I'm not going to be a Pollyanna and plague you by saying that what happened was all for the better, but do not discount your own suffering in all this. Hasn't that, in part, been responsible for this achievement?

And he might have felt some elation if he had read no further into her present life, her husband's (an accountant with his own business) and her son's, and now a second pregnancy—all of which weighed. He was glad for her, but envious and resentful of his failure and loss; but after several days of festering, he overcame his self-pity—the pain of that long ago, unforgotten day, since which he had sought Sue in each woman—he decided to call Sue in Colorado.

"Congrats from a long-lost friend."

"Mark! You're *here*?"

"No, no. I'm in Madrid. Your letter came, and I wanted— I guess really I felt like talking—to say—well, you *know* what I feel—and how thrilled I am for you—again."

"And we're thrilled. Josh can't wait. He wants them even more than I do, and you know how badly I do."

As I did. Do.

"In some ways he reminds me of you, Mark. I hope that doesn't offend you."

"On the contrary, I'm flattered. That, in fact, makes me feel all of me has never left you."

"But of course it hasn't. How could it? Everything we've ever done's in us."

"Everything," he said.

"Then—?"

But he did not speak.

"If it's a boy, it's David. If it's a girl—they say it is—we'll call her Ariadne."

Silent, he felt happy, sad, resentful, lonely.

"Mark? Mark?"

"Yes?"

"You're at it again. I know those silences."

"Yes."

"Don't. You know yourself. You *should* be able to reckon with your—"

"Defect?"

"Yes. Why shouldn't you?"

"It's easy to say."

"No, it's *not* easy, not for me. But someone—you—should say it. Haven't you told yourself a hundred times—you should have, and I'm sure you have, but what time is a crucial time?—that you have a defect. We all have in one way or another, and why should you be any different? Why should you feel special in all creation? Isn't that nothing but pride pushed to the limit?"

For a moment he felt a knife pierce, but she was so *Sue*, so blunt, direct, unrelentingly honest, that he had to laugh. He laughed loud.

"*Yes*, that's it," she said. "Laugh. You should. If it's not funny, it *is* comic in the best sense. *You've* said often enough we have to protect ourselves by laughing—if it doesn't cure, it helps."

He laughed again. "I didn't call for a moral lesson."

"And I didn't have one in mind when you called."

"Thanks. Say hello—and congrats—to Josh. And David. And, oh yes, Ariadne."

"You!"

"Adiós, Sue."

Who in Hell Do You Think You Are?

Because it was hot, Rosario, he wanted to say after. And it was no lie. It was sweltering, and underground in the Metro, two escaltors down—he was on the way up to La Latina—with the hottest blow. He was sweating. There must have been a major concert in the sports arena: from deep below he could hear the yells and laughter of a mass of young people pouring from the train and mounting the escaltors. Bandying jokes and laughter, up them came, running, leaping steps, trying to outdo one another; dodging, jostling, causing comment and cries from adults. They laughed at the old, rebuffed with insults.

"Don't shove!" an old woman cried. "*Maleducados!*"

"*Mierda*!" somebody shouted. The others laughed, moved past, poking, chain shouting, indifferently thrusting people aside, pegging one another until all poured into the corridors.

And he was late, irritated by the noise and heat. Thank heaven Rosario had a saint's patience, and the tickets—she loved those dated Spanish comedies of Arniches, pure escapes into the illusive comforts of yesterdays, and she never missed the comic Saza if she could help it. If anything, what *he* needed was a comedy. When almost caught up in the turmoil of teens passing through the corridor, he moved out of the current at the San Millán exit and the raft of them disappeared, he came up against one coming down and headed straight at him. He couldn't avoid the boy, who struck him head on. He hit the wall. Stunned, he stared at the boy—but only an instant; then with abrupt fury he struck , struck, struck till the boy—he *was* a boy despite the beard, long hair, slack rankled clothes, eyes and mouth too firm and mean. "Yes," he *swore*, "mean, Rosario." When he saw the wallet in the boy's hand, then his own hand had no mercy— *Because of the heat*, he wanted to tell Rosario, "as if, Rosario, my hand *wanted* to kill him, it hit and hit—" And before he could know, someone was gripping at his hand, pulling it back, and one arm trying to grip his waist to hold him off the boy—"Ay, hombre, please, por favor, you'll kill him"—and at the same time he tore, tried to tear, free—failed—and fell on top of the boy. "And me thinking, Rosario—this is the horror!—thinking *Yes, I'll kill him*, and at the same time seeing the boy's arms, the marks and scars, and thinking with an absolutely unfamiliar kind of liberation—yes, an unexcelled freedom, *I swear*, a kind of ecstasy to let go, beat him, kill—and with that sudden inexcusable reasoning *He's an addict, a dope addict.* I'm sure I repeated it again and again as I struck him, the other man pulling me back, shouting 'Please, please, señor, you'll kill him.' The wallet was lying on the dirty cement now, the boy bleeding but still lashing out, yelling I can't remember what, maybe just sounds, the boy free now as the other fell back with me in his arms, holding me till the boy got up, crawled, ran—after, I could see the blood from where he'd guided his way along the corridor to the market exit. And I stood there, Rosario. The man—he was young—helped me, almost stood me there and held me up. 'Are you all right? Can you walk? If you feel dizzy, I'll walk you to a cab.' I stared at him, Rosario. It struck me like a seizure what I'd done. That boy! How I had hurt that boy who in no time had vanished and would no doubt be running for his life, skulking, to hide in some part of the city alien to me. And I was ashamed. I could hardly face the man beside me, kind, who should have beaten me with some kind of eye-for-an-eye justice, but who was absolutely *bondadoso*, who understood more than I might have if I had been that man then. That's the *horror*, that it was *not* someone else, it was me, and *I* had betrayed that someone else. I could hardly face that other man. I thanked him but turned from him, ashamed, knowing even in his understanding he too must have felt shame for me, even *with* me, and maybe even for *himself*, Rosario, as another person with *my* impulses, as if he understood because he knew what I was experiencing—and more, what that boy—addict or no, apart from whatever caused it, whatever need—was experiencing. That's what shamed me most of all. I thought, *Who the hell do you think you are, to want to—to try to kill—when you are dedicated—you* say *your whole life is dedicated to . . . life. Rosario,* I thought. *How will I ever explain this to Rosario?* Then I thought *But she'll understand, she'll know—*

"I swear I could have died at that instant because I saw *me* there, *me*—and not in that boy's hands as he was in mine—but *me* in my *own* hands, *me* beating *me*— I told that man 'I'll be all right, just let me sit here on the steps for a minute, to rest,' and he said 'You're sure?' and I said, 'Yes, yes. You have been very kind. I don't need help. The boy is the one who needs help.' But it was too late for that, though *he* agreed, 'Yes. I hope he is not badly hurt,' and I said, 'Yes. He must be all right, he must be,' and the man nodded, silent then, and left with, O God, a pat on my shoulder. I sat there thinking again, *Who in hell do you think you are!* with a kind of prayer that that boy somewhere was already breathing better, walking better, standing better, on his way to feeling *I will make it, I will be okay,* and *me* thinking with an anguish like thunder in my blood, both in shame and with a strange kind of exultation, even a perverse joy, that I had beaten on myself, flagellated *me*. I was not only ashamed but at the same time startled at the discovery—what I had beaten in him was me. By beating him I'd beaten me *alive* to the very thing I was ashamed I'd tried to kill in him—this: me, you, Rosario, everybody. That boy made me know. I want my self. I want all my selves, Rosario."

H. E. Francis is the author of ten previous books, over two hundred stories, and numerous translations. His stories have been included in the *Pushcart, O. Henry*, and *Best American Short Stories* volumes. His book *The Itinerary of Beggars* won the Iowa School of Letters Award for Short Fiction, and his book *Naming Things* was selected for the Illinois Short Fiction Series. He taught for many years at the University of Alabama and received three Fulbright fellowships to Argentina. He now divides his time between Hunstville, Alabama, and Madrid, Spain.